Fern MICHAELS

GOLDEN LASSO

Silhouette Books

Published by Silhouette Books
America's Publisher of Contemporary Romance

SILHOUETTE BOOKS

GOLDEN LASSO

Copyright © 1980 by Fern Michaels

ISBN 0-373-48297-3

This edition published by arrangement with Harlequin Enterprises B. V.

® and TM are trademarks of Harlequin Enterprises B. V., used under
license. Trademarks indicated with ® are registered in the United States
Patent and Trademark Office, the Canadian Trade Marks Office and in
other countries.

Printed in U.S.A.

Available from Fern Michaels

Golden Lasso
Beyond Tomorrow
Paint Me Rainbows

Chapter One

Janice Warren shook her shining chestnut curls with a mixture of sadness and relief as she scrutinized the legal paper before her. The stiff, crackling letter, if she was interpreting it correctly, held the answer to her and Benjie's future.

"What's wrong, Jan?" the little boy in the bulky wheelchair asked fearfully, not understanding his sister's sudden silence. "Did the doctors say something scary about me? Is that why you look so funny?"

"Of course not, silly," Janice soothed, wiping the tears from her eyes. "This letter is going to make everything right for you and me. Do you remember Dad's brother? Uncle Jake? He owned the ranch in Arizona.'' At Benjie's nod, she continued, ''Well, he left the Rancho Arroyo to me, and I'm going to share it with you. That's the happy part. The sad part is that Uncle Jake died and no one notified us. The letter says that he wanted a simple funeral. Uncle Jake was like that—fiercely independent.''

With nine-year-old logic, Benjie asked, ''How come he left the ranch to you? Didn't he have any children of his own?''

''Uncle Jake's wife died when she was very young and they had no children. I guess we're the last blood relatives and Uncle Jake was big on family.'' Janice blurted over a sob, ''Oh, Benjie, do you know what this means? We can go to Arizona and begin a whole new life. I remember your doctor telling me there was a marvelous clinic in Phoenix that specializes in problems like yours. We've never been able to afford it; but now, since we'll be living close by, we can! You can go there and they'll help you and pretty soon...''

''I'll be able to walk again!'' Benjie shouted happily, tossing his dark tousled head, his blue eyes shining.

''With God's help, that's exactly what's going to happen. I can't wait to see you out there playing Little League ball with all of the kids again. And you will,'' Jan said with determination. ''I'll see to it if I have to work twenty-four hours a day to make it come true.''

"What about your job here and that boyfriend of yours, Neil Connors—the one who doesn't like me?'' Benjie asked curiously.

"Benjie!'' Jan cried in surprise. "What a terrible thing to say. What makes you think Neil doesn't like you? And as for my job—pooh, I didn't like it anyway.''

"I heard Neil say you were going to be saddled with me for the rest of your life, and he didn't plan on taking on a kid brother. I heard him,'' the little boy said past a lump in his throat.

"Well, if you heard that then you must have heard my reply. You did, didn't you?'' she asked anxiously, her green cat's eyes studying her brother.

"No, I didn't hear what you said. I sort of... I thought Neil might tell you to put me in an orphanage or something.''

Jan was off the chair and kneeling in front of Benjie. "Hey, this is Jan, your big sister. I thought we had an agreement that if something was bothering one of us we could talk it out. How could you think such a thing? I told Neil that you and I were a team, and if he didn't want to be part of that team, then that was his problem. I told him when Mom and Dad died in that car crash and you managed to survive I swore that I would take care of you for the rest of our lives. I meant it, Benjie. All we have is one another, now that Mom and Dad are gone. And now that Uncle Jake is gone too, we're all that's left of the Warren family. We have to stick together. You're such a good little kid putting up with me and never complaining when other kids are out there playing and having a good time. You're going to play, too—you have my word on it. When we get to Arizona, you'll get lots of fresh air. There'll be horses and treatments at the medical center, and at night you're going to be so tired you'll sleep better than ever. What do you say partner? Is it a deal?" Jan asked huskily as she hugged the little boy.

"You bet! When are we going to leave? What about my schoolwork?"

"We'll leave at the end of the week. Tomorrow is going to be a very busy day. There're only three weeks of school left before summer vacation, and I doubt if it will be a problem since you're a straight A student. I'll make the plane reservations this evening and start packing our gear. We'll just close up the house and decide later if we're going to keep it or sell it."

"Tell me about the ranch, Jan. Did you ever see it?"

"Once, when I was about your age, maybe a little older. It's great, Benjie," Jan said enthusiastically. "The main building is made from logs and there're all kinds of planters with bright flowers at the windowsills. There were separate cabins for the guests—a dozen or so, if I remember correctly—and each of them is on what Uncle Jake called a trail that branches off the main path. He wanted his guests to have privacy so they're sort of scattered. When it was in season, he would have big barbecues, where he roasted a whole steer, and then have a square dance. The guests would wear cowboy outfits, and there was an old Indian who played the guitar. At that time he had a lot of really good horses that he kept for his own pleasure and others that were for his guests to ride. All of the people who worked for Uncle Jake seemed to love him because he really cared about them. It was homey and cozy, and I guess that's what I liked about it. Mom and Dad went there on their honeymoon, and I guess that makes Rancho Arroyo special, too. I hope we can make a go of it—I don't know the first thing about running a dude ranch. This letter," Jan said, tapping the legal paper, "says the reservations for the guests have all been confirmed and we're starting off with a full guest list. The first party of guests arrives the day after we do. Our worries are over, little brother," Jan cried exuberantly. "I'm going to pack some of my things now. Do you want to come upstairs or would you rather watch television?"

"I'm going to work on my model and sort of listen to the TV if that's okay with you."

"Sure. If you want me, just holler," Jan said, running lightly up the stairs. Once she was inside her room she unfolded the letter from Uncle Jake's attorney and reread it. It was the last paragraph of the letter that bothered her. The printed words sent a chill down her spine as she reread the ominous-sounding words.

At the moment I doubt there is much cause for alarm; however, I feel that I must alert you to the fact that a new dude ranch, owned by Derek Bannon, had just been opened in the same vicinity. It caters to the entertainment crowd and its specialty appears to be a Las Vegas atmosphere. Your Uncle Jake was concerned up until the end about the effect of such a place on his little enterprise. However, he believed that family atmosphere and good home cooking at Rancho Arroyo would win out. I want you to be aware, Miss Warren, that while all the reservations have been confirmed, there is nothing that says a guest can't change his mind once he sees the glittering Golden Lasso. I want you to be prepared for any and all emergencies.

I feel it is imperative that you visit my office as soon as possible upon your arrival, as there are many facets of the business that need discussing.

Jan folded the letter carefully and placed it in the zipper compartment of her handbag. The Golden Lasso. A man named Derek Bannon. Jan's stomach curled into a hard knot. Suddenly, she was afraid. Could she handle it? She had to, for Benjie's sake and for her own. She had wept so bitterly that day at her parents' grave site when she promised to take care of Benjie. She wouldn't let a man named Derek Bannon upset her plans—not now, not when Benjie's welfare was at stake.

From time to time, as Jan busily packed and sorted and then discarded, she caught a flash of her reflection in the long mirror in her room. Was that grim, tight jaw hers? Of course it was—she was being threatened by an unknown named Derek Bannon. She could feel it, almost taste it. Benjie's future was being threatened more than her own. But now it was time for her to call the airlines and make their reservations. And she did it with all the calm she could muster. The die was cast. She would make a go of the ranch; she had to. Now she had to call Neil and tell him what was happening.

After putting the receiver back in its cradle, Jan applied a light layer of makeup around her eyes and then deftly added a little color to her cheeks. She couldn't give way to her feelings now, especially not in front of Benjie and Neil, who, rocked by the news that she was leaving, was due to arrive any moment now.

But it was Benjie with whom Jan was concerned. The youngster was so attuned to her feelings he could sense immediately if something was wrong. She had to think positively and act confidently in front of the little boy.

With trembling hands, she ran a brush through her short-cropped chestnut curls. She frowned at the smattering of freckles that ran across her nose and then winced as she thought of the effect the Arizona sun would have on those hated freckles. Her mother's comforting words, "Jan, don't worry about your freckles. With those gorgeous emerald eyes of yours, no one will ever notice them," didn't help now. Twenty-one-year-old women weren't supposed to have freckles. Neil always poked fun at her freckles, but in a nice way. She supposed she would miss Neil when she went away, but Benjie was more important to her than romance. Not that there was much romance—not with her obligations to be both mother and father to Benjie. But still, Neil had always been in the wings waiting for her to have time for him.

Jan scowled. Romanticizing already? Face the truth, she told herself. Neil is great; he's nice to me, and he's always ready to give me a hand when I need it. He has a good job and he'd good-looking— a great catch, as the other girls in the office had told her. But somehow Jan couldn't stir herself up over a great catch. And the fact that she was willing to drop everything and go out to Arizona was proof enough to her that Neil just wasn't that important in her life.

There were times when she had thought he was about to ask her to marry him. But something always held him back. There were times, also, when Jan was so tired and disgusted with trying to make ends meet and taking care of Benjie that she knew that if Neil had only said the word she would have married him in a minute. It would be nice to have someone to lean on, she thought. But then, at other times, when she seemed to have control of the situation and she was well rested, she knew that marrying Neil would be a mistake. There was something lacking in their relationship, something she sensed in Neil that didn't appeal to her. Or was it because she knew Benjie didn't like him?

Neil Connors wasn't the kind of man who could make the earth move under her feet, Jan decided. At best, Neil might be able to move a small hill.

Jan descended the stairs calmly. It was time for Benjie's medicine and his snack before bed. She watched him toil away with his model and marveled at the child's patience. He held the tweezers and the tiny sticks that held pinpoints of glue on the end and matched them perfectly. He looked tired, poor little kid, and yet he never complained. He just sat and waited till she had time for him. He looked just like their father with his crisp, dark hair and bright blue eyes. Even now, at the age of nine, he had their father's chin, complete with a small cleft. He was bright and precocious with a delightful sense of humor. She loved him dearly. He was all she had left, and there was nothing or anyone who was ever going to change that. Not ever.

Benjie was at the kitchen table, his wheelchair pulled up close against the edge, when the doorbell rang insistently. Neil. Jan opened the door and in he stormed.

"What do you mean you're going off to Arizona?" he demanded, pushing his fingers through his thick blond hair.

"Just that," Jan railed. "And if you'll give me a minute, I'll explain it all to you. Come on into the kitchen and say hello to Benjie. I was just going to put him to bed. I'll pour you a cup of coffee."

Jan turned back to the kitchen, Neil hot on her heels. "Explain!" he demanded again, not bothering to answer Benjie's polite "Hi."

As Jan poured his coffee, she began to explain, feeling her patience fail. Was Benjie right about Neil not liking him? She shrugged and handed Neil his coffee. "C'mon, Benjie. Ready for bed? I'll be right back, Neil. Make yourself at home."

"Can't he get into bed on his own, for chrissakes?"

"Yes, he can," Jan bristled. "But when you were nine years old, didn't you like to have someone tuck you in?"

Jan returned from the downstairs den, which had been made over into a bedroom for Benjie. "Whatever you do, keep your voice down," she told Neil. "He's going to find it difficult enough to get to sleep."

"Yeah, yeah, okay. Now, what's this all about?"

Slowly, Jan explained, watching the look of disapproval deepen on Neil's face.

"You mean you're just going to go out there and take over and run that place?" He laughed harshly. "What do you know about running a dude ranch?"

"Nothing. No more than I knew what it was to run a house and take care of a little boy," she retorted sharply. "But I learned real fast. And I don't think the idea is so ridiculous. I'm not stupid, you know."

"I never said you were stupid, Jan. Just inexperienced. Naive. You're going to lose your shirt— you know that, don't you?"

"Thanks for the vote of confidence. No, I don't know that I'll lose my shirt. There are people out there, Neil—my uncle's staff—who know all about running the ranch. And am I or am I not one of the best darn bookkeepers you know? I'm halfway through my courses to become a certified public accountant, and that takes brains, whether you like to admit it or not."

"All right, so you're not stupid. But going off to Arizona this way is! What about your life here? This house? Your job?" He slammed his coffee mug down onto the table, sloshing coffee onto the checkered cloth.

"In that order? My life in Arizona would be a change from the humdrum life I live here. The house? I was hoping you'd keep an eye on it for me. My job? I've already told you I'm not stupid. I can always find a job. But what's most important to me is Benjie. There's a clinic out in Phoenix that was recommended to me months ago, but I couldn't afford it. Now Benjie will have the opportunity to go there and be helped."

"So that's who's behind all this. That kid." Neil stood up abruptly and put his cup in the sink.

"Benjie is my brother, Neil, not 'that kid.' And no, he's not behind this. I would have taken this opportunity anyway. Benjie only validates my reasons for moving on this so quickly. I'm sorry you feel this way, Neil. I was hoping you'd cheer me on."

Neil looked at Jan, an expression of exasperation on his face that clearly stated that this was the dumbest move she could make. "Write out a list of instructions about the house. I'll take care of it for you. When did you say you were leaving? Don't bother telling me—I don't want to know. Leave the list of instructions in your mailbox. Goodbye, Jan."

Without turning around or saying another word, Neil pushed open the kitchen door and stalked out. Jan sat down moodily. Whatever reaction she had expected from Neil, this definitely wasn't it.

Jan was thrilled by the attention Benjie received on the plane from the stewardesses. On boarding, the pilot had handed the little boy a pair of plastic wings, and at the last moment he had fastened them to Benjie's polo shirt. Benjie had beamed his thanks, and from time to time Jan watched him touch the pin during the long trip.

Benjie was happy and amenable to this change in their lives, trusting Jan to take care of him. For a moment tears blinded her. She knew she was guilty of being too maternal, too protective of him. She was going to have to let go in degrees. In New York it had been hard, but now that they were going to the wide-open spaces, perhaps she could manage to bring herself to relinquish her hold and let others have a chance at getting to know the little boy. He needed friends—good friends—who would love him as she did. They were making the right move, Jan told herself determinedly—she was sure of it.

Besides, the house in upstate New York would be there for them if things didn't work out. Her cushion, so to speak. Now, with the income from the

ranch, she wouldn't have so much difficulty meeting the taxes and insurance payments. And the
money for Benjie's treatments wouldn't be so difficult to come by. She admitted she had become
bone tired from holding down two jobs: her regular one at the dairy, where she was a bookkeeper,
and her evening job as a receptionist at a health
spa. Benjie's care hadn't presented a problem because he was at school all day while she worked at
the dairy, and then at night he had been allowed to
come with her to the health spa. Still, he had gotten to bed late, and more times than she cared to
remember, they had eaten cold suppers from her
lunch bag. But he had thrived and hadn't lost
weight, and that was important, according to his
doctors. What Benjie needed was her love and the
security only she could provide.

Other niggling little thoughts plagued Jan as she
stared out at the fluffy clouds far below them.
What about me? the contrary little voice demanded. When am I going to have a life of my
own? A chance to go out on dates or just for a simple dinner? For the past two years she hadn't even
been able to accept an invitation. It was no wonder
Neil had been so grudging of Benjie. What kind of
date was it to sit and watch television after Benjie
went to bed? And she had always been firm about
ushering Neil out at the stroke of eleven. She didn't
have much going for her either way she looked at it.

Dreamily, Jan closed her eyes and let her mind wander. It must be wonderful to be in love and thrill to another's voice. To know that the person loves you as much as you love him. Would she ever have the time to find that elusive thing called love? Would she ever be free to accept that love? She was almost twenty-two and so far it hadn't found her. She admitted she wanted to be swept off her feet. She wanted, yearned, to feel someone's arms around her, and she wanted to be kissed till she was left breathless and wanting more.

A sound of light laughter, feminine and crystal-sounding, captured Jan's attention. Across the aisle sat a fashionably slim, stylishly dressed woman about Jan's age. Her long, slim legs were crossed, and when she turned her head Jan saw that she was very pretty. The man sitting beside the woman seemed very attentive and kept glancing at her appreciatively as he spoke to her. Whatever he had said to her seemed to strike her as amusing and she laughed again, a light-hearted, abandoned sound that wrenched at Jan's heart. How long had it been since she had been carefree and laughed that way?

"...but I'm going to be married before the month is out. Do you think it would be right if I met you for a drink?" The woman's voice was light and teasing as she flirted with the good-looking, massively built man beside her. "It was only coincidence we took the same flight to Phoenix.... And my fiancé is rather jealous..." The rest of her statement was lost in the sound of the jet engines.

Jan watched the girl across the aisle covertly, a frown of scorn drawing her finely arched brows together. She didn't think much of any girl who could so lightheartedly announce that she was engaged to be married and at the same time flirt so blatantly with the first stranger she met on a plane. A jealous, green monster nipped at Jan's sense of propriety. Some girls just seemed to have it all—money, looks, someone who loved them—and still it didn't seem to be enough. A sudden rush of pity for the girl's fiancé forced Jan's pretty mouth into a thin, straight line.

"As long as you promise to behave yourself," the girl in the aisle warned. "I don't suppose a little drink would hurt anyone. I'll be at the Golden Lasso..." Again her words were drowned out as she turned her head away.

At the mention of the Golden Lasso Jan jumped to attention. Over the top of Benjie's head she took another long look at the girl and sighed. Women as beautiful as that always had men dancing attention around them, she concluded. Jan stiffened her back and sat up straighter in her seat. This was definitely none of her business, and she should be thinking about the kind of reception she would find at Rancho Arroyo and in what condition she would find it.

"I think we're going down," Benjie said, his eyes wide as he stretched to peer out the window. "Look, Jan, the seat belt sign just went on. Is someone going to meet us?"

A knot formed in the pit of Jan's stomach. This was the beginning of a new life for the both of them. She was the new owner of Rancho Arroyo. Boss lady. She could handle it—she would have to. Taking a deep breath, she leaned back and readjusted her seat as the stewardess requested. Quickly, she pressed the button on Benjie's seat, raising it to a full sitting position, and smiled at how happy he was. She had originally thought he would be terrified of flying. But nothing could have been farther from the truth. Benjie took to flying like a duck to water.

As the airport came into view and she felt the jar of the mechanism lowering the landing gear, Jan said a silent prayer that the Rancho Arroyo would be a happy place to make their new home and that the medical center in Phoenix would be successful in helping Benjie to walk again. She was tempted to utter a small plea to grant her wish for love and romance and then changed her mind. That would be almost too much to wish for.

Once on the ground, Jan peered around the airport baggage area searching for a person who looked like they might be looking for her. Surely,

Uncle Jake's attorney had told someone at the Rancho that Benjie was in a wheelchair. If they didn't recognize her, Benjie was certainly visible with his hundred-watt smile.

Chapter Two

"Miss Warren? It is Miss Warren, isn't it?" a drawling voice inquired.

"I'm Jan Warren. Are you from Rancho Arroyo?" she inquired of the tall, slim man in the tight Levis who was towering over her.

"You've got it, and this little guy must be your brother. Andy Stone," he said, holding out his big, sun-bronzed hand to Benjie, who shook it manfully. "See that man over there?" he asked, motioning to a tall, dark-skinned man standing near the luggage carousel. "That's Gus and he's full-blooded Cheyenne Indian. He's the man who's going to take your baggage to the van and then we're all going to the ranch for a proper welcome."

"Wow! A real Indian!" Benjie cried excitedly.

Jan smiled, "Thank you for that, Andy Stone. I really appreciate it." She handed him the baggage tickets.

"He looks like a nice little kid and it must be rough being glued to a chair like that. I have a little brother in Montana who isn't much bigger and I...what I mean is...Heck, ma'am, I'm just rattlin' on. But your little brother is going to be around people who really care about young ones."

Jan smiled brightly and alleviated Andy's embarrassment. "Look, Andy, there's a man who seems to be trying to get your attention."

Andy tilted his head and looked in the direction Jan was indicating. His mouth tightened and his eyes narrowed. "That's Derek Bannon—he owns the Golden Lasso. There must be someone important on this plane if he's here to meet him personally. You might as well know now before someone else tells you—he's approached everyone who works at the ranch to come and work for him. Some of the people he asked directly and others he sent his business manager around to them. I was one of the ones he approached directly. I turned him down flat. It was hard because he offered me quite an increase in wages. But I liked your Uncle Jake. He took me in and gave me a job when I needed it, and I don't forget that quickly. Looks like Bannon's coming over here. Let me handle it. Later, when you're up on all the goings on, you can take a shot at him yourself."

Jan was bewildered. Fifteen minutes on the ground and already she had a problem. Instinctively, she trusted Andy Stone. Her own gaze narrowed as she watched the tall, muscular Derek Bannon make his way through the milling passengers who were waiting for their luggage. He was tall—taller than Andy Stone—and he wore his extra flesh well. There was nothing lanky about Derek Bannon. He maneuvered himself gracefully, like a cat, and his low Western boots had just the right amount of shine to them. His Levis fit to perfection as though they were tailor-made, as did the shirt he wore, open to reveal a massive, sunbronzed chest. There was a slight curl to his crisp, black hair and just a trace of gray at the temples. Steely blue eyes stared at her and through her, making her feel uncomfortable.

"Have you given my offer any more thought, Stone?" he asked Andy in a deep voice that seemed to come from somewhere in his chest. His eyes, however, were on Jan.

"Not today, I haven't. I've been a little busy. This is Janice Warren, the new owner of Rancho Arroyo, and her brother, Benjie."

"Miss Warren, a pleasure." Jan knew he noticed that she hadn't extended her hand, and after a moment he turned his attention to Benjie. He held out his hand and Benjie grasped it and shook it heartily. "Benjie, is it? How old are you?" Derek Bannon asked.

"Nine on my last birthday, sir."

"Isn't it time you were called Ben instead of Benjie?"

Benjie flushed and stared at Jan and then at Andy Stone.

"But that's my name. My mom and dad gave it to me. They're dead and I can't change it, can I, Jan?"

"If you want to. Your real name is Benjamin and Benjie is just a nickname, like Ben. You don't have to decide right now, Benjie, and it isn't important. Is it, Mr. Bannon?" she asked in a cold tone that told the man it was none of his business what her brother's name was.

Derek Bannon shrugged. "Perhaps we'll see one another again." With a curt nod, he weaved his way through the milling crowd.

"What a strange man," Jan said in a puzzled tone.

"He's more than strange, Miss Warren. He's a hard man to fight, and believe me when I tell you you have a fight in store for you. He wants your ranch and he's not going to stop until he gets it."

"I like him," Benjie chirped. "I liked the way he didn't stoop over and pretend I was a little kid. And I liked it when he said I should be called Ben. I liked him," Benjie said emphatically.

"Well, will you look at that!" Andy said in surprise, pointing to a group of men. "That's the entire Bison football team, and I guess they're staying at the Golden Lasso." Benjie's eyes boggled at the sight, and Jan didn't miss Derek Bannon wave his hand in the little boy's direction.

Jan tugged at Andy's arm. "Why does Mr. Bannon want my ranch?"

"Beats me, Miss Warren. All I know is he wants it. He was forever palavering with your uncle, and as far as I know Jake turned him down each time."

"Is our ranch a threat to the Golden Lasso?" she asked fearfully, afraid now that all her wonderful dreams were going up in smoke.

"I can't see how. Our clientele is different. We cater to families with children. Good home-cooked food, fresh air, and family-type entertainment. Bannon, on the other hand, is all glitter and frills. He's got show girls at the Lasso that would put some of those Las Vegas girls to shame. I don't mind telling you the people around here were just a mite disturbed over the whole thing. But then they all settled down nice and quietlike when they saw the Golden Lasso held pretty strict standards."

"Why would Mr. Bannon want to open a resort way out here in the first place? Why not Las Vegas?"

"Derek Bannon inherited the land from his father. Over two thousand acres. The only piece he doesn't own is the five hundred acre spread the Rancho Arroyo is on. Your Uncle Jake won that piece in a poker game from Bannon's father. He wants it back. Unless you're one hell of a poker player, I don't hold out much hope for you. Money talks, and Derek Bannon talks big. But for what it's worth, I'm on your side, Miss Warren."

"If you're on my side, then I want you to call me Jan. Is it okay if I call you Andy?"

"It's a deal, Jan. Looks like Gus is getting restless; I'd better get these baggage claims over to him. Then what do you say we mosey on back to the ranch?" He swaggered, pretending to be a cowboy, much to Benjie's delight. "Gus, now—he doesn't talk much, but he listens. There isn't much that goes on around here that he doesn't know about. A body would be hard pressed to try to pull the wool over his eyes," Andy said softly to Jan before he left to help Gus with the bags.

"Andy," Jan stopped him in midstride. "Did Derek Bannon try to wean Gus away too?" she asked anxiously.

"You used the right word. Try was what he did. Gus listened and didn't utter a word. Oh, he was

polite about it. After Bannon had his say, Gus just
spit tobacco juice in the road and moved on. It's
just a guess on my part, but some of the other
hands back at the ranch figure that Bannon wanted
to exploit the fact that Gus is Cheyenne. You
know—dress him up in feathers and paint or
something.''

While Andy took Benjie over to the luggage carousel, Jan scanned the airport. Her eyes immediately fell on the escalator, where she saw the girl
who had sat across from her on the plane. Now that
she was standing, Jan could get a good look at her.
The first thing she noticed was that she was alone;
apparently, she had said her goodbye to the man
seated beside her on the plane. Second, Jan could
see what a terrific figure she had. Tall, slim, and
willowy, wearing a clingy jersey dress that set off
every curve to an advantage. And her shoes! Just
how some women learned to walk in those sky-high
creations was beyond her.

Suddenly, it seemed as though the girl spotted
someone, and before the escalator touched bottom
she lifted her arm and waved in excited greeting. As
lightly as a dancer, she was off the escalator and
skipping across the floor right into Derek Bannon's arms.

Jan was staggered. The girl had spoken about
being engaged to be married. Could her fiancé be
Derek Bannon? From the way he was hugging

her—swinging her up off the floor and twirling her around—it must be. For an instant, Jan felt smug. Well, Mr. Bannon, it seems as though Rancho Arroyo isn't the only thing you can't put your brand on; your little girlfriend was making a date with another man. But the thought had a bitter taste.

Benjie demanded her attention. "Hey, Jan! Come on! Andy's bringing the van around to the front. Let's not keep him waiting!"

During the ride to the Rancho, which was about forty miles outside of Phoenix, Jan was entranced with the countryside. She remembered the beauty of the desert from her last visit to Arizona, but it hadn't seemed so majestic through the eyes of a little girl. Now she could view the shifting sands and the arrow-straight road with amazement that so close to a burgeoning city there could be such wilderness. Low mountain ranges lifted the horizon, and in the late afternoon the sun painted myriad color schemes from dull reds to vibrant purples with each scheme punctuated by black shadows and low-growing scrub. There was peace here—Jan could feel it—and she knew it was a sight she could enjoy for the rest of her life. Instead of becoming tired, her eyes picked up every nuance of color and symmetry. Gus, too, seemed intent on the scenery. Since climbing into the van beside Andy, his gaze never strayed from the window except to glance at Benjie to see how he was faring during the ride.

From the interstate highway Andy pulled onto a secondary road following a beaten signpost that pointed the way to Rancho Arroyo. "It's about four miles after turning off the interstate. That's where your property begins. From there, on our own road, which we maintain, it's another two miles. Think it's too far from civilization for you, Jan?"

"There were some days in the big city, Andy, that I thought the moon wasn't far enough away. Where's the Golden Lasso from here?"

"Well, you follow this secondary road for about eight or nine miles, and you can't miss it. It's only about two and a half miles as the crow flies, though. The roads are indirect to say the least."

Jan watched through the windshield and gained her bearings. They had headed west out of Phoenix and now were heading north. As Andy turned into the private road leading to the ranch, Jan's heart pounded with excitement. And when they at last pulled through the split-rail fence and she saw the low, flat buildings of her new home, she nearly shouted with joy. It hadn't changed. It was still the same. And she loved it.

"This is really beautiful." Jan drew in her breath. "I had remembered it being this way, but I was afraid to see that perhaps it had become run down with use and age. You see," she offered Andy by way of explanation, "it's been a long time since

I was here. Not since I was a child not much older than my brother. It's just perfect." She eyed the colorful window boxes. "I know we're going to be happy here, don't you, Benjie?" But Benjie was off, his chair skimming over the smooth flagstone patio, Gus close behind.

"Don't worry about the boy—he's found himself a guardian. Gus loves kids, although you'd never think if from his rough exterior. Come on inside and meet your staff." Andy held the screen door open.

The dimness inside startled Jan for a moment after the bright light of day. But she recovered quickly and took in everything around her. The heavy pine tables were polished to a high gleam and the long, low leather sofas and armchairs looked inviting. The plank wood floor was buffed to a patina and Indian print scatter rugs seemed to follow the traffic flow and make intimate little conversation areas, almost like rooms within the room. The ceiling was rough adobe sectioned off by rough-hewn beams, and the far walls of the lobby were covered with used brick on which were hung gleaming brass plaques that offset the huge round wagon wheel chandelier with its brass lanterns. And everything sparkled—not a hint of dust anywhere, not even on the various plants and ferns showcased against the walls and positioned around the vast room. Off to one side of the door was the desk, and behind it the numerous nooks and crannies for mail and keys. Behind the desk was a door, and through it she could see a small, cozy office with one window that looked out on the corral. Her office, Jan told herself—her very own office.

She didn't hear the woman until she was standing beside her; she was wearing leather moccasins. Jan was looking down at the oval braided rug and knew it was handmade.

"You like." It was a statement, not a question. "I make it many years ago for your Uncle Jake."

"This is Delilah, Gus's wife. Don't ask me where she got the name." Andy grinned.

"Hello, Delilah." Jan smiled. "I understand you're our chef."

"I cook, I clean, and I do everything. You like my name, Delilah? I pick myself. Gus no Sampson, but I am Delilah," the woman chortled.

Jan liked her immediately. She was small and round as a ball with shiny black eyes and a wealth of braids arranged on her head in a coronet. Deep laugh lines etched Delilah's face, and Jan thought her one of the most beautiful women she had ever seen. "I like your name very much. It shows you have character," she told Delilah seriously.

"You see," Delilah said, poking Andy in the ribs. "One smart lady, Jake's niece. But you skinny like stick," she turned back to Jan. "One week, two, and I make you like Delilah.'' Jan pretended mock horror as Andy swooped her out of the lobby.

"Bannon offered Delilah a fantastic sum to come and work for him,'' Andy said sourly.

"But you said Gus turned him down. Surely Delilah wouldn't go without her husband.''

"I hate to be the one to tell you this, but we only have Delilah's word that she's married to Gus. Gus doesn't commit himself one way or the other. Every now and then Delilah gets it into her head to try to make Gus jealous. He yanks her hair and gets her back in line until the next time. But she loves bangles and beads, so keep it in mind. You can buy a lot of doodads with the kind of money Bannon is tossing around.''

"I'll keep it in mind. Let's do the tour so I can go into the office and get familiar with the way things have been done around here.''

"If those books are anything like the way your Uncle Jake did everything else, you'll find them in top order. I thought maybe you'd wait until that lawyer from Phoenix came down to give you a hand with them.''

"Don't worry about me, Andy. I've been a bookkeeper since I graduated from business college. I think I can handle them. Then you do know where they're kept?''

"Sure, everybody knows. There's a safe behind the desk and the combination is the numerical value of the word *Jake* in the alphabet. You know, A is the number one and so on. So working left, right, left, it's 10-1-11-5."

Jan smiled up at Andy. "Is there anything you don't know about the Rancho Arroyo?" She laughed.

"Oh, I suppose there's a few things." He seemed embarrassed and pulled the brim of his Stetson low over his eyes.

"Seems like my Uncle Jake trusted you, Andy Stone. And I'm giving you fair warning—I'm going to trust you too." Seeing a flush of color creep up from his shirt collar, Jan changed the subject. "Are you sure Benjie is okay?"

"He's fine. By now he probably has every ranch hand on the place eating right out of his hand. Little kids are kind of hard to resist around here, and he's automatically special if Gus adopted him."

They followed the main path down to the first trail leading to the cabins, where she followed Andy across the planked verandas and stepped inside. Every modern convenience had been installed in the cabins: air-conditioning, tiled baths—even a little efficiency kitchen. Some of the cabins were one-bedroom, but most were two-bedroom affairs, capable of housing a family with children. And each was furnished in Western flavor with heavy oak pieces and bric-a-brac and were kept in A-1 condition.

"There's a lot of work that goes into housekeeping around here. Who does it all?" she inquired.

"There's four women who come in on call when they're needed," Andy explained. "They live on the outskirts of Phoenix and make the drive in every morning. As for repairing fences and the like—you know, roof repair and painting and taking care of the stables and horses—that's what the ranch hands do to keep themselves busy. They're a good bunch of guys, Jan, and I know you'll like them. Between myself and Gus, we handle things during the offseason. Right now, you've got a full crew working for you. Delilah has two girls to help her in the kitchen and she rides herd on them. Come one, I'll take you down to the corral where you can meet the hands. On the way we can stop at the swimming pool."

By sundown Jan had taken her tour and had a bath and a cup of coffee. She pored over the account books until her eyes ached. Everything was right side up. Now all she had to do was keep it that way. A small cash flow, an emergency fund, a filled reservation list, and a storeroom full of every supply known to man—she couldn't ask for more.

At first she had been surprised and then relieved to discover that liquor was not served on the ranch. Applejack and a liberal dose of that potent liquor called white lightning was kept in the locked storeroom, and each had a label that stated it was the property of Gus: "Keep Hands Off."

After dinner she took Benjie and settled him down in bed after his long, exciting day. With guests arriving in the morning, she wanted to be fresh and clear-headed when she handed over the first key to her first guest. She couldn't wait and she knew she would have trouble dropping off to sleep. She only hoped that thoughts of Derek Bannon and his faithless fiancée didn't keep popping into her head the way they had all during the day.

Chapter Three

Jan watched the sun come up from her room in the lodge. The sight was breathtaking. Only once before had she seen anything its equal and that had been a sunrise in Key West, Florida. She toyed briefly with the idea of waking Benjie and quickly negated the thought. There would be other days, other sunrises, for the little boy to see.

Benjie occupied the room adjoining hers on the second floor of the lodge. He had been as thrilled with his room as Jan had been with hers. She loved the dark mahogany furniture and the tall, heavy-paneled chifforobe that stood sentry just outside her private bath. Even here there was a flavor of days gone by. The floor was covered with an Indian patterned rug, and the walls were covered with a small-scale print of cranberry on federal blue paper. The bedstead was huge, and she had found the night before that she had had to literally climb into it. But the mattress was firm and the sheets smelled sweet, and she had almost immediately dropped off to sleep.

As Jan made up the bed and smoothed the dull cranberry comforter, which doubled as a spread, she wondered how she could feel so comfortable in a room completely devoid of the frills and ruffles she had had back home in New York. This room was handsome, almost masculine, the only feminine items being the Victorian globe lamps on her night tables. But comfortable it was, and it seemed to fit her new way of life. There was an austerity about it that seemed to compliment her new position of authority.

Jan washed and dressed herself in a comfortable pair of jeans and a long-sleeved blouse. As she stepped into a pair of wedge-soled clogs, she vowed to buy herself a pair of Western boots, and almost giggled at the thought. She didn't want to seem like a weekend cowboy, but she knew that the boots would do double duty against the hard-packed roads and trails leading to the various cabins. She would be covering a lot of territory on foot each day and she needed serviceable shoes.

She raked a brush through her chestnut curls and blessed the fact that her hair was naturally curly and, worn short, didn't require much attention. She'd be too busy from now on to fuss with elaborate hairdos. A last look in the pier glass, and Jan appreciated the fact that her jeans were well worn and didn't look new, as though she were contriving to look the part of a ranchowner. She liked the way they felt against her skin and admired the way they fit. They had been worth every saved penny she had paid for them.

A glance at her watch and she sighed. She would have to awaken Benjie and get him ready to come downstairs. It seemed a shame to wake him from his sound sleep, but there was no help for it. Benjie required a considerable amount of diligence to get him out of bed, washed, dressed, and into the wheelchair. After she had him ready, Gus would come up and carry him down the stairs to his chair. It hadn't been so long ago since Benjie hadn't been able to do anything for himself, but since he had gained the strength to maneuver on crutches, things had improved. But he still needed help in pulling up his trousers and tucking in his shirt. Jan smiled. Soon, with heaven's help and a lot of work, Benjie would be totally self-sufficient; but, she reminded herself, he would probably still need help to get him to wash behind his ears.

Breakfast was a perfunctory affair, with Jan being too nervous to eat more than a few bites of toast and drink several scalding sips of the best coffee she had ever tasted. She itched to get behind the desk in the lobby and wait for the Marshall family, which was to arrive at 10:00 A.M. She had it all planned. First she would greet them and register them in the large book on the desk. Then she would personally escort them to Cabin Six on Wayward Trail. She hoped they would like the seclusion and the scent of scrub pines that surrounded the three-room cabin. And after that she would drive into the Phoenix Medical Center with Benjie for his first treatment. She knew that was going to work out right also. It had to—it just had to!

Before leaving New York and on the advice of Benjie's physicians, she had phoned the Phoenix Medical Center and spoken to Dr. Rossi, who would take over Benjie's case. In her suitcase up in her room was Benjie's medical file, which she would give to Dr. Rossi. There had been a lot of preparation involved in having her brother continue therapy in Phoenix, and it was important that he not miss his first appointment.

A cup of lukewarm coffee at her elbow, Jan waited at the desk, her patience barely under control. It was now after eleven and Andy still hadn't returned with the Marshalls from the airport. She looked around the inviting lobby and was sud-

denly apprehensive. Surely nothing was wrong, but
if the Marshalls didn't arrive soon, she was going
to have to leave with Benjie for Phoenix.

She saw the dust and then heard the van. Even to
her inexperienced ears, it sounded as though
something was wrong. It hadn't coughed and spit
like that yesterday when Andy and Gus picked them
up at the airport in the minibus they used to trans-
port guests to and from the city.

Andy looked disgusted when he ushered the
Marshalls into the lobby with their luggage in tow.
While Mr. Marshall filled out the registration card,
Mrs. Marshall oohed and aahed over the plants and
copper and brass and kept rein on her two precocious little daughters. Andy took Jan aside and
whispered. "There's something wrong with the van.
I'm going to have to call a mechanic out from town
to take a look. Usually Gus tinkers with the wheels,
but this is something with the transmission. We
might have to tow it into the garage. We can use the
pickup truck around the ranch so we aren't en-
tirely without transportation. Hopefully, the mechanic can repair the van before tomorrow, when
the other guests arrive. If not, we'll have to hire a
limousine. Sorry."

"But, Andy, I have to take Benjie into Phoenix
for his first therapy session this afternoon. Can I
use the pickup? What about a taxi?"

"I don't recommend the pickup. It's old and it's been patched up so often with spit and prayers, it's apt to conk out on you two miles down the road. A taxi is out unless there's a fare coming in from the city. I guess you're going to have to cancel the appointment. I'm sorry, Jan. Where do you want me to take the Marshalls?"

"Cabin Six on Wayward Trail. There must be something I can do," Jan almost wailed. She had forgotten that she wanted so desperately to take the first guests to their cabin but it was too late. Now all she wanted was to get Benjie into Phoenix.

"Perhaps I can be of some help. I couldn't help overhearing. I'm going into Phoenix and would be more than happy to take Ben with me," Derek Bannon said quietly.

Jan was stunned by his sudden appearance. Where had he come from and what did he want? He looked so physically fit, Jan felt weak and ineffectual beside him. His tan was just the right blend of bronze and gold, making his blue eyes brighter by contrast. Again, she was uncomfortable with his nearness. Should she accept his offer to take Benjie into Phoenix. Would he feel imposed upon? Would it make her indebted to him? Especially when he discovered that Benjie's therapy sessions took over an hour and he would be obliged to wait. She decided she would hold her answer until she discovered what he really wanted.

"Is there something I can do for you, Mr. Bannon? I know you didn't come here just to offer us a ride into Phoenix."

Derek Bannon's blue-eyed gaze was openly amused and faintly mocking. "As a matter of fact, I did come here on business. I never beat around the bush. I want to buy Rancho Arroyo from you."

"I never beat around the bush either, Mr. Bannon. Rancho Arroyo is not for sale. Today, tomorrow, or any other day."

"Name your price, Miss Warren, and I'll have a check drawn within the hour," Derek Bannon said arrogantly, ignoring her reply.

Anger shot through Jan. "From reports I hear about your establishment I know that Rancho Arroyo couldn't compare to that glittering palace, and why you would make an offer for this ranch is beyond me. I plan to run this ranch and make a go of it. It's my and Benjie's home now, and one doesn't sell one's home on a whim. It's not for sale, Mr. Bannon," Jan said coldly.

"Everything is for sale if the price is right," Derek answered without emotion. "It might interest you to know that I was negotiating with your uncle, and we had about come to terms before he passed away. As I understand it, he died within minutes of suffering the heart attack. It was his intention to turn the ranch over to me."

"That's not the way I heard it. My people tell me my uncle rejected all three of your offers, and this makes your fourth rejection. Rancho Arroyo is not for sale, and, contrary to your opinion, everything and everyone does not have a price. Including me."

Derek Bannon leaned over the desk, the masculine scent of his after-shave making Jan's senses reel. He was so close Jan could have counted his eyelashes. Gently, he cupped her face in his hand and drew her closer to him. She knew his lips were going to touch hers, and she made no move to withdraw. Instead, she stared deeply into his eyes, aware of the intensity she saw there. It was a light kiss, feathery and fragrant, and left her feeling awkward and wanting more. This time she did withdraw. "Kissing me, Mr. Bannon, is not going to get me to sell you this ranch. At the risk of repeating myself, I can't be bought." To her own dismay, her voice sounded breathless and husky, betraying the fact that she was more affected by his kiss than she cared to admit.

Derek Bannon's eyebrows lifted and a wry smile touched the corners of his mouth. "Everyone and everything has a price. One just has to find it. Now, do you want me to take your brother to Phoenix or not? I'm leaving almost immediately."

"I can't be ready that soon," Jan said curtly. "I'll have to find another way to get into the city."

"You didn't understand me. I didn't ask you to
go. I offered to take your brother. Dusty Baker, the
running back on the Bison football team, has to
have hydrotherapy on his knee. I thought your
brother would enjoy riding along and meeting
Dusty. I'll wait for him while he has his treatment
and bring him home safe and sound."

Tears burned Jan's eyes, turning them into glittering shards of green glass. "Benjie isn't for sale
either, and I think it's rotten of you to try and get
to me through a little boy."

"It doesn't matter to me what you think, Miss
Warren. I offered to do you a favor. Take it or leave
it," Derek Bannon said coolly, his eyes shooting
white sparks of anger.

Jan knew she had no other choice. Benjie's appointment was important and she couldn't just
cancel it because everything hadn't gone according
to plan. Benjie propelled his chair through the
lobby, and she watched as his eyes lit up at the sight
of Derek Bannon. "Benjie, Mr. Bannon has offered to take you to the medical center along with
one of the football players. Do you think you can
handle it?"

"Wow! Sure, Jan. Really, Mr. Bannon, just you
and me and one of the Bisons?"

"Dusty Baker," Derek replied, watching Jan's
face.

"Dusty Baker! Jan, did you hear that? Gosh, he's my favorite player! Is it all right, Jan? Huh?" Benjie literally glowed with excitement.

Jan couldn't find her voice, but she nodded her agreement. "Just remember, Mr. Bannon," she finally managed through clenched teeth, "Benjie is a little boy who has gone through traumas even an adult couldn't handle. You hurt him in any way and you'll answer to me."

"That sounds like a threat and unworthy of such a pretty lady." Derek smiled.

"That's not a threat, Mr. Bannon, that's a promise."

Derek laughed, a rich, booming sound that seemed to fill the room and bounce off the walls. "I make it a practice never to offer advice, but I'm going to make an exception this time. Don't ever threaten me, or you might get more than you bargained for. And stop smothering the boy with your frustrated maternal instincts. He's going to have to make the best of whatever life has in store for him. Find yourself a cat and take your frustrations out on it."

"You . . . you arrogant, insufferable . . ."

"You ready, Ben? My car is out front. I'll meet you there," Derek said, striding through the open doors.

Benjie sensed Jan's intention of helping him. "I can do it, Jan. If Mr. Bannon thought I needed help, he would have offered. I can do it," Benjie insisted manfully as he turned the chair and expertly propelled it through the doorway without touching the wooden frame. "What did I tell you?" he called over his shoulder.

"Yes, I see," Jan said weakly. "I'll be right down with your medical file. Don't leave without it." Quickly, before she could change her mind, Jan ran up the stairs and dug into her suitcase for his records, then raced down the stairs.

Outside, Benjie was already situated in the car, his wheelchair folded in the back seat. She handed Benjie the manila envelope and turned to Derek Bannon. "You don't know the name of Benjie's doctor or where he's supposed to go."

Walking toward her, he grasped her arm and almost dragged her back into the lobby. He stood facing her, hands on hips, a look of disgust on his face. His voice was laced with sarcasm when he spoke. "Miss Warren, don't ever take me for an idiot. There's only one doctor at the center who can give the therapy your brother needs. And he's the same doctor Dusty Baker must see. I happen to know Dr. Rossi personally, and he mentioned to me that your brother was coming in for treatments. He felt it would be convenient for him if Dusty came in at the same time."

Again the words stuck in Jan's throat. He was insufferable. It had been natural for her to offer

instructions as to where and whom Benjie was to
see. After all, Derek had just popped in out of no-
where and had taken matters into his own hands.
He certainly seemed like a man who had all the answers—and then some.

It took Jan the better part of an hour to get her
emotions under control. There was no point in
denying that Derek Bannon had an effect on her.
He made her aware of the fact that she was a
woman, a woman with feelings that had been sub-
merged too long and were now creeping to the surface. She felt suddenly alive and vibrant. She liked
the feelings and wondered what it would be like to
be held in his strong arms and to feel his heart
beating against hers and to know a deeper kiss than
the feathery touch he had pressed upon her.

Jan felt herself blush. What was wrong with her?
Derek Bannon was engaged to be married to that
beautiful woman she saw on the plane. And what
kind of person was he to kiss her and stir these
emotions in her when he had promised himself to
another woman?

And what kind of woman was Derek's fiancée to
have someone like Derek Bannon dancing on a
string while she amused herself with other men? A
fool, that's what she is, Jan thought hotly. Derek
Bannon was the kind of man to answer most girls'
prayers, and there was his fiancée playing him for
the fool. Or was that the normal way of doing

things in that kind of glittering, glamorous society that the Golden Lasso suggested? Was that the kind of morals those rich and beautiful people had? Well, it wasn't *her* way—not in the least. If she ever pledged herself to someone, she'd never amuse herself with flirting with other men. And she'd never, never be attracted to a man like Derek Bannon, who probably collected women the way other men collected stamps.

Why did some men think they were so clever? Didn't Derek realize she saw through his little plan? He would try to make her brother his ally, his friend, and he would state his demands again, once he had the boy wrapped around his little finger. Well, he wasn't going to get away with it. This was one of Benjie's relationships that she was going to nip in the bud.

The remainder of the afternoon was spent in meeting the housemaids and inspecting the linens and supplies. When she visited the stables, she developed a particular affection for a mare named Soochie. She promised herself she would brush up on her riding techniques and take the gleaming palomino out for a canter at the first possible opportunity.

From time to time Jan heard the Marshall children squeal in delight over their father's antics in the swimming pool. When she glanced at her watch again, she was appalled to see that it was after four o'clock. Benjie should have been home by now. Each session was only an hour. A smidgeon of worry shot through Jan. What if Derek Bannon had forgotten the little boy and left him there at the medical center? What if they had had an accident? What if…what if…scurried through her brain until she gained control of herself. Her face flushed a brilliant scarlet. Derek Bannon was a responsible man, and he truly liked her brother. Whatever else he may be, he was reliable, and she knew she could trust him with Benjie's care and safety.

Jan was busily working her way down to her third fingernail when she heard the high-pitched whine of Derek Bannon's sports car. She waited a second and then walked out onto the front veranda. The sight of Benjie's weary face went straight to her heart. Poor little guy, he looked so beat, and she hadn't been with him to help, if not with physical support, at least to cheer him on. Quickly, she opened the car door, intending to scoop Benjie into her arms and croon over him as their mother would have done.

"Don't! Ben can manage." It was an iron command, an order not to interfere. Jan stepped back in alarm, fearful that something was wrong with Benjie. Her eyes pleaded and implored the man in front of her to say something to reassure her. He said nothing, did nothing. Instead, he waited for Benjie to look up.

"What do you say, Ben? We can do it two ways. I can help you or you can help yourself," Derek said quietly, but encouragingly.

Benjie grinned. "If you push the chair closer, I think I can handle it, Derek."

Bannon gave the chair a little nudge with his foot and waited. The little boy slowly maneuvered himself to the edge of the car seat, his lower lip caught between his teeth. He slipped and Jan made a move to reach out a supporting hand. Derek Bannon caught her arm in a viselike grip and held firm. Benjie righted himself and slipped into the chair. "I did it!" he cried jubilantly.

Jan was suddenly aware that the man hadn't released his hold on her arm, although his grip had loosened. She liked that touch and hated the man. He was sadistic. "That was a brutal thing you just did," she hissed. "He's such a little boy, and he's absolutely exhausted. Why couldn't you help him or, at the very least, let me help him?"

"He didn't need any help. Leave him alone before you destroy him." Without another word, Derek slid behind the wheel of his car. His powerful hand moved effortlessly over the gear shift as he expertly reversed the sports car. "By the way, Dr. Rossi suggests you give him a call the first of next week. Benjie has a pamphlet describing the exercises he's to work on before his next visit to the center. And I suggest you get him out into that swimming pool. It's the best thing for him.''

Benjie called, "Thanks, Derek. Thanks for taking me to the hospital.''

Derek Bannon waved without turning around to acknowledge the boy's goodbye. He was insufferable!

"I'll bet you're starved. How about a snack like we used to have at home. Tea, cheese, and crackers?''

"I'm not hungry. Derek and Dusty took me for tacos and I had two with a malted. Isn't he great, Jan? And Dusty Baker is a super guy—just the way he looks on television. He didn't talk to me like I was a little kid. We talked about plays and signals and he said I knew a lot about football. Derek is going to take me to the field behind the Golden Lasso to watch the Bisons work out tomorrow. He said you could come along if you wanted. I told him you hated football and wouldn't want to come. You don't, do you?'' he asked anxiously.

Jan felt deflated, and defeated by Derek Bannon. And yet Benjie, who was usually so reserved with strangers, liked him. Maybe she was missing something.

"Look what Derek gave me,'' Benjie said pridefully, rummaging in his jeans pocket. "Four tickets to the Bisons salute dinner. I'm not sure what a salute dinner is, but Derek said I should get you to bring me. Can we go, Jan? Huh?''

Jan inspected the white cards with the gold engraving. "Benjie, these tickets cost one hundred dollars each! I can't afford to buy them.''

"They're free, Jan. Dusty gave me two and Derek gave me two. The other two are for Andy and Gus.''

"We'll see,'' Jan said, not wanting to make a decision at the moment.

But Benjie was not to be put off. "Don't, Jan. Just say yes or no. I don't like it when you tell me maybe,'' he said quietly.

"My 'maybes' never bothered you before,'' she answered tartly, knowing who she had to thank for Benjie's sudden independent behavior. "I want to remind you that you're only nine years old, and I'm the one who is taking care of you. It has to be my way, not Derek Bannon's way. Do you understand?''

"I understand, all right. I understand that you don't like Derek. Well, that's okay, too, because I heard him say he didn't like you. He told Dusty Baker you were on the verge of being a frustrated old maid,'' Benjie said with all the force he could muster. Mouth pressed into a grim line, he turned the chair and headed down the driveway.

Tears trickled down Jan's cheeks as she watched Benjie's slow progress in search of Gus. Things were falling apart, and they had only been on the ranch for twenty-four hours. What had she done to deserve those biting comments from Benjie? All she wanted was to love him and see that he was well again. Hadn't she given up two years of her life for him since he had been injured? And Derek Bannon swoops into their lives and it's all for nothing. Now I'm not good enough for Benjie. Whatever I can do, Derek Bannon can do it better. "In a pig's eye!" Jan snarled as she stamped her foot on the blacktop. "No way, Mr. Bannon!"

Still smarting from Benjie's comment on being an old maid, Jan made her way to the tiny mailroom and began to sort through the mail. She was just on the verge of taking it back to her office when Delilah intercepted her. The little Indian woman was carrying a large wicker basket. "This come for you on a special truck. Man wait for money. Says is five dollars and two cents."

"Are you sure it's for me? I didn't order anything. What is it?" Jan asked as she dug into petty cash for the money to give Delilah.

"How should I know? You open, we both see." Delilah waited patiently. "Will you open before I pay man or after I pay man?"

"I'll wait for you to pay him," Jan muttered. "I have no idea what it could be. I'm certain I didn't order anything."

It was Delilah who finally opened the wicker basket lid. She cocked her head to one side and peered into the basket, her shoe button eyes merry and full of mischief. "This funny present. I think you get stung. Is not worth five dollars and two cents. Must be tax, too?" she said authoritatively.

Swallowing hard, Jan moved nearer the basket and looked inside. A cat! Of all the unmitigated gall! Arrogant, know-it-all playboy! And she had paid money for it! He was cheap in the bargain!

Delilah's eyes widened. "You want cat? We have many for free in barn. You think maybe this is special cat?" she asked inquisitively.

"Nope. This is your run-of-the-mill, everyday alley cat, and from the looks of things she's about to bestow a blessing on us. Here, Delilah, you can have it," Jan offered generously.

"You pay, you stuck with present. Even for free, I don't want it. Maybe in New York you pay for cat. Here is free. You make little mistake but all right. Next time you look inside before you pay," Delilah indulged.

"There isn't going to be a next time. I should take this cat to the Golden Lasso and demand that...that..."

"He good-looking man, no? He make me itch all over." Delilah giggled as she waddled from the room. In spite of herself, Jan laughed. She would send Derek a thank you card that would set his teeth on edge. Better yet, she would send him the whole kit and kaboodle after the litter arrived.

Before getting into bed that night, Jan penned off a letter to Neil telling him all about Rancho Arroyo. She carefully omitted the fact that the minibus was out of order and that she had had a confrontation with the owner of the Golden Lasso, who was a stiff competitor for business. She did describe the landscape and the wonderful condition of the lodge and the cabins and the beautiful Arizona sunshine. Silently, Jan crossed her fingers and hoped that the trouble with the minibus and the disarming situation with Derek Bannon weren't an omen of things to come.

Hastily, before she was tempted to confide in Neil, she licked the envelope and pressed it shut.

Chapter Four

Jan saddled Soochie and rode out past the ranch into the wild terrain. Paying careful attention to the direction she was taking, she watched for the blazed trail and fence posts that would lead her around the entire circumference of Rancho Arroyo.

It was a beautiful day and promised to be hot, with the sun scorching down on the parched land. Yet there was beauty to be found here, so different from the verdant appeal of the Catskill Mountains with which she was so familiar. Here the eye could stretch, following the low, uninterrupted land right out to the horizon, where, in the distance, purple mountains stood sentinel and lifted the eye to the vibrantly blue sky. It was still early—hours before the heat of the day—and Soochie seemed grateful for her escape from the corral.

Relaxing in the saddle and instinctively trusting Soochie's temperament, Jan gave the palomino free rein. There was time to enjoy her new home now that everything seemed to be running smoothly—on the surface at least.

Andy had taken the guests on a ride into the desert and wouldn't return until well after sunset. A campfire and a sing-along was planned for them before their return to the ranch. She made a mental note to be on hand for the nine o'clock pool party, complete with Delilah's scrumptious buffet goodies.

However, Jan was aware of vague undercurrents that had recently reared their ugly heads. A mantle of worry settled over her slim shoulders as she dismounted and tied Soochie's bridle to scrub pine. She sat down on the hard-packed earth and munched on the cheese and crackers she had thought to bring along. Andy's grim words that the van could not be repaired without a major overhaul on the transmission had been the last thing she wanted to hear. But when the mechanic discovered a cracked engine block, the world seemed to come to an end. The ranch would have to buy a new minibus. Momentarily, she had panicked. To pay cash or take it on time payments was a difficult de-

cision. She had finally opted for cash because the
dealer was offering her a sizable discount if she
took it that way. Her small cash reserve was now
seriously depleted. And if Andy was right about the
air-conditioning unit in the lodge going on the fritz,
she was going to have another gigantic bill facing
her very soon. She couldn't very well expect her
guests to eat in a hot, stuffy dining room and her
guests wouldn't expect it either.

Jan leaned back against an outcropping of rocks,
her hands trembling. Was it the bills or was it the
fact that two of the ranch's prospective guests had
changed their minds about staying at the Rancho
Arroyo once they saw the glittering Golden Lasso?
There had also been three future reservations for
large families that were also canceled. At the moment they weren't in any serious difficulty and
could weather the storm, but if there were any further cancellations, the ranch could bury itself in the
red side of the ledgers. A devastating thought, especially since Benjie would soon be ready for his
third treatment.

And to make matters worse, while the guests
professed to adore Delilah's cooking, Jan had noticed that most of them preferred dressing up and
going to the Golden Lasso for dinner and entertainment, leaving their children behind for her and
her staff to tend to. There wasn't a thing she could
do about it. And all the food that Delilah prepared

was wasted because there was no one to eat it. Jan groaned and her stomach churned at the thought of the colossal waste of food every day. From the looks of things, there wasn't going to be any profits for a long time to come.

And then there was Derek Bannon. Each time she saw him she felt more drawn to him and more confused than ever. Clucking mother hen indeed, she sniffed. A lot he knew and what business was it of his anyway? He'd just better not think he was going to make any decisions where Benjie was concerned. She was his own sister and she knew best.

Tears of self-pity burned her eyes and she brushed them away with the back of her hand the way Benjie did. It seemed she was doing an awful lot of crying lately. Maybe I am a frustrated old maid, she thought sadly. A man kisses me and I go all to pieces. As if that kiss meant anything to me. I've got other things to think about. Like earning a living for myself and Benjie. There's no time to become attracted to anyone—especially not a man like Derek Bannon.

Jan was about to gather up the crumpled cheese and cracker wrappers when she noticed her feet were in shadow. She had been so involved in her thoughts she hadn't heard him approach.

"Littering, Miss Warren? And trespassing," Derek Bannon said mockingly.

Jan was acutely aware of her position: sprawled on the ground, her legs wrapped in faded jeans and tucked beneath her like a yogi. She felt the trail of scarlet begin in her neck and work its way up to her cheeks. Her hateful freckles must be lighting up like neon lights, she thought inanely. She should say something—anything—to wipe that know-it-all smile off his face, but the words stuck in her throat. Scrambling to her feet and belatedly remembering the papers in question, she bent over like a child who had been severely reprimanded and stuffed the cellophane into the pocket of her jeans. She was humiliated and embarrassed and knew Derek was reveling in it. She hadn't seen the girl astride the cinnamon-colored horse waiting behind the scrub. Jan's eyes widened. It was the girl from the plane— Derek's fiancée.

The girl sat upon her horse looking like a model with her precision-cut clothes molding her slim body. She sat comfortably in the saddle as though she were born to it, and the soft, white Stetson was worn on the back of her head with just the right amount of ebony hair showing in front.

Jan had envied the girl on the plane, had been shocked to learn in the airport, that she was Derek's fiancée, and now she knew she could hate her—especially when she called to Derek in a low and husky voice.

"Andrea, I'd like you to meet our new neighbor. Miss Jan Warren," he said coolly, "who owns the Rancho Arroyo. This is Andrea, my..."

Before Derek could complete the introduction, the girl's eyes widened. "Really! So you're Jake Warren's niece. And is Ben your son?"

Jan stared first at Andrea and then at Derek. "Yes," she answered airily. "I really am. And as for Benjie, I'm more what some people would call his clucking mother hen," Jan snapped as she slid her foot into the stirrup.

At first Jan thought she had imagined it, but Derek was grinning at her. "Touché," he said softly.

"I'm sorry if I trespassed and I did clean up my litter, so I presume I'm free to leave." It was plain to see Derek was enjoying her discomfort.

"Don't move, either of you," he said suddenly in a strangely hoarse whisper.

Jan looked in the direction of Derek's gaze and then she saw it at the same time Andrea's horse bolted and raced off. A coiled rattler had crept out from beneath the rocks. She gulped and tried to swallow as she watched Derek rein in her horse and lead it carefully away.

"Aren't you going to kill it?" she asked hesitantly, fighting back her own urge to bolt and run.

"You may have noticed, I don't make it a practice to carry my six-shooter," he answered sarcastically. "Besides, the Western rattler is an endangered species, and for the most part they're more frightened of us than we are of them."

A shudder ran through Jan. "I'm afraid of snakes and bugs," she babbled. "Thank you. Andrea—is she all right?"

"Andrea was born to the saddle. By now she's back at the Golden Lasso with a Bloody Mary in her hand. Here, let me help you—you look a little shaky."

"I'm all right," she snapped as she threw her leg over the saddle horn to slide to the ground. If there was one thing she didn't need at the moment, it was Derek Bannon's help, for that would require that he touch her, and then she would fall into his arms, weeping with fright.

She fixed a deliberate haughty expression on her face and slid from the saddle. Soochie sensed the change of weight upon her back and daintily backed up, throwing Jan off balance. Derek reached out his long arms and drew her against him.

Suddenly, she felt safe, protected, and it was with great difficulty that she forced herself to pull away from his grasp. She couldn't allow this arrogant man to see what he did to her.

"Your palomino is still a little skittish; give her a few minutes before you try to ride her," Derek said softly as he lowered his gaze to meet hers.

His blue eyes, shaded by the brim of his Stetson, had a hypnotic effect on Jan. It seemed, when she looked up at him, that all she could see was the blue sky framing his powerful shoulders and his face. Soochie was forgotten and the world seemed to tilt, and, like a moth to flame, she was drawn into his arms. For a long moment he looked down into her upturned face, and Jan was tingling with expectancy. His hand cupped her face, his long fingers coming to rest on her neck beneath her ear. Finally, at last, and with determination, he brought his face closer, touching his lips to hers. With an urgency that left her breathless, his arms closed around her, holding her against his lean, hard strength, and his mouth becoming more demanding, crushing hers, insistently summoning a response.

Derek Bannon filled her world. The sheer strength of the man, the wide width of his shoulders, the flaming touch of his mouth on hers became her existence. There was no world, no anything, beyond the reach of his arms and the touch of his lips. He was gentle, he was insistent, he was demanding, he was tender.

A rush of emotions pummeled her senses and the earth seemed to move beneath her feet. Jan clung to him, lifting her face to his, answering his demands, filling her own. He brushed the hat from her head, and his hands were in her hair as his mouth sought hers.

Jan felt her sensibilities leave her, and in their place, from somewhere deep within, came an answering response. As though of their own volition, her arms sought the rippling muscles of his back, the narrowness of his waist. Her thighs pressed against his, feeling their strength through the fabric of her jeans. He was no longer kissing her, and she was aware that his breath came in sharp rasps that matched her own. A deep sound of pleasure escaped him as he began to trail his lips along her neck and then down to the cleft between her breasts. Jan clung to him, welcoming him, pressing herself closer.

Derek Bannon smiled down at her. "Tell me you didn't like that."

Jan bristled, and with a huge effort she managed to regain control of herself. "Oh, I liked it, all right," she managed to say tremulously, "but you kiss like you do everything else—to perfection. The next time—if there is a next time—try putting some emotion into it. We clucking mother hens not only want, we demand, warmth and feeling. And, Mr. Bannon, I'm still not for sale and neither is my ranch."

Derek's face was set into grim, hostile lines. "Perhaps there's something lacking in you, Miss

Warren. I've kissed many women, and you're the first who has complained.''

"I'll just bet you have—kissed lots of women, that is," she snapped, thinking of Andrea. "And that makes you one up on me because I haven't kissed many men. But I do know what I like and what I don't like. Perhaps the reason no one has ever complained is because they're like you. Peripheral, without depth, no emotions. In short, Mr. Bannon, I find you sadly lacking.''

Quickly, she mounted Soochie and dug her heels into the animal's flanks, riding off and leaving a stunned and angry man looking after her.

Soochie seemed to be aware of the emotions that embroiled her young rider. Jan's trembling hands couldn't control the reins, making the palomino skittish and unruly. How in the world had she managed to let him kiss her? And where in the world had she mustered up the nerve to say the things she had said? The full weight of the situation descended on her, seeming to block out the sun and chill the air. Liar. Jan Warren is a liar, a small voice hissed. You loved it, you loved every minute of it and you know it. Liar. Liar! You just didn't want him to know that he shook the earth beneath your feet.

Jan's backbone stiffened and she railed against the small voice. "He deserved it!" she shouted to the sky. "He's going to marry Andrea, and he thought he could play his games with me! He deserved it!'' Still, on the long ride home Jan couldn't seem to erase the memory of his lips on hers or the way his hands touched her hair. And the soft sound of pleasure that came from him when his mouth found the soft flesh between her breast came back to her.

At Rancho Arroyo Jan was greeted with a broken air-conditioning unit and a mean, angry Gus, who was stomping around the lobby as though he wanted to kill. Benjie was watching the man with wide eyes, uncertain if he should maneuver his chair out of Gus's way or not.

''What's wrong? Will someone tell me what's happened? If whatever it is is going to cost me money, please, tell me gently. Where's Delilah?''

''That's what the problem is,'' Benjie whispered. ''She quit and went to work for Derek at the Golden Lasso. She just left a little while ago. You should have asked her to stay,'' the little boy accused the tall Indian.

Gus continued his parade around the lobby, stopping once to light a foul-smelling pipe. He puffed furiously as he stomped out his anger.

''If Delilah is gone, who's going to prepare the buffet table for the pool party?''

''There isn't gong to be any pool party tonight, so we don't have to worry about the buffet,'' Benjie volunteered. "One of the ranch hands drained the pool and forgot to turn the water back on."

Jan sat down and wished she smoked so she could light a cigarette. Instead, she jumped back up and headed for the storeroom and uncapped a jug of Gus's white lightning. She took one gulp and recapped the bottle. She waved away the fumes and thought that flames were going to shoot from her mouth any second. When nothing happened, she locked the storeroom and made her way back to the stiflingly hot lobby.

"Well, Gus, aren't you going to go to the Golden Lasso and fetch Delilah back where she belongs?" Jan asked irritably, her throat burning from the alcohol.

Gus favored her with a withering glance and continued his furious pacing.

"Why?" Jan asked, throwing her hands helplessly in the air. "How could you let her go like that? The ranch is without a cook and I can't even begin to cook for all these guests. Gus," she implored, "we need Delilah."

"Delilah said Gus doesn't make her itch and she's tired of not listening to him. She said he never says anything," Benjie offered sadly, knowing he was going to miss the little round woman who made apple tarts for him with globs of icing on top the way he liked them.

"Then I'll go myself and get her," Jan said huffily. "I appreciate her even if you don't, Gus."

"Mr. Bannon won't give her back to us. Delilah said he was going to lock her in his kitchen and never let her get away. That's what she said," Benjie said at Jan's look of disbelief. "Honest."

"Where's the pickup? I'm going to get her, and when you see me again, Delilah will be with me. You can count on it or my name isn't Jan Warren. Will you come with me, Gus?" He just continued with his furious pacing, which was becoming wilder by the moment. "Well, if you won't come with me, do you have a message to her you want me to deliver?"

"Yes," Gus replied. Jan was dumbfounded. She had been at the ranch over a week, and it was the first time she had heard him actually speak. "Tell her I'm not itchy," he said in perfect English.

"That's just exactly what she's going to want to hear," Jan said stormily as she flounced out of the lobby and went in search of the battered pickup truck.

She seethed all the way to the Golden Lasso. More than one scathing look was shot her way in the parking lot of the Lasso. The truck was definitely not Lasso material among the Cadillacs and Continentals, not to mention the Mercedes that peppered the ample parking area. Jan looked around and made her way to the back of the club.

No sense causing more of an uproar by going in the front door. She flinched when she remembered Andrea's perfect attire. The Lasso's hired help probably dressed better than she was at the moment.

Jan found the kitchen by the aroma. Delilah must be making her specialty—corn bread with raisins. She stood for a moment and watched the small woman wipe at her eyes from time to time. Quietly, Jan opened the door and stood a moment till Delilah recognized her. "Delilah, please, you have to come back to the ranch. I'll pay you whatever Mr. Bannon is paying you. You can't let me down now. There's no way I can possibly cook for all the Rancho's guests. If you stay here, I'll have to send them here and refund their money."

"I make promise to Mr. Bannon. I give my word," Delilah said defiantly.

"That's wrong, Delilah. You gave me your word when I came to the Rancho that you would stay and work for me. If it's Gus who's bothering you, you have something you better learn right now. He will not come over here to get you. He belongs at the Rancho, and if you stay here he's . . . he's going to get another . . . well, what he's going to do is find himself a . . . a girlfriend, and then where will you be?"

"You think Gus do that?"

"Pirating my help, Miss Warren?" a cold voice inquired.

"Actually, you could say I was pirating my help *back* again. That was a pretty shabby, shoddy thing for you to do, Mr. Bannon. Your tactics are definitely to the left of Attila the Hun," Jan said in a furious, choked voice.

"A simple business proposition. I offered Delilah money and she accepted. What's wrong with that?"

"There's nothing wrong with a simple cut-and-dried business arrangement, but it didn't happen like that and you know it. You're trying to put me out of business and it isn't going to work. I'm not selling and that's final!"

"My dear Miss Warren, think whatever you will," Derek Bannon quipped. "You're trespassing for the second time today."

"Yes, I know, but I came to talk to someone. So I consider it fair for me to be standing in your kitchen. Delilah, are you coming with me?"

Delilah looked uncertain, and from Jan's vantage point it looked like Derek Bannon was going to win. Jan felt desperate. "Delilah," she pleaded, "think of Benjie. What's he going to do, Delilah? He's such a little boy and he needs you. I need you."

"Okay, I come," Delilah said, taking off her apron. Without a backward glance, she followed Jan from the spacious kitchen. Jan allowed herself a smirk as she sailed past the astonished Derek Bannon. "And that's what I call fair."

Jan backed the pickup from the parking slot and headed for the highway. She took her eyes from the road a minute to look at Delilah. "I'm glad you're coming back with me."

Delilah shrugged. "I thought Gus come for me. I not plan on staying there. At Rancho I big boss in kitchen. At Golden Lasso, many cooks. Chefs, they call themselves." Delilah sniffed her disapproval of their self-appointed titles.

Jan was silent on the drive back to Rancho Arroyo, grateful that she had succeeded in getting Delilah to come back to work. And then it hit her. It had been too easy. Men like Derek Bannon always won. If he had wanted to keep Delilah, he would have kept her, and no amount of pleading on her part would have changed things. Men like Derek Bannon did not get where they were in the business world by being nice to their competitors. Suddenly, she felt like a fool. She had been maneuvered by an expert, and she had fallen for it. He was giving in graciously now; later, when she was lulled into a false sense of security, he would strike another blow in his quest for her property. Her hand trembled on the steering wheel. She felt uncertain, betrayed somehow. The only certainty on the horizon was that Derek Bannon wanted her ranch, and if he had to ruin her in the process, he would.

Jan shivered in the hot, dry air. If that was so, then she would go down fighting. Derek Bannon would at least know he had picked a formidable adversary. She had to wait and play the waiting game just as Bannon was doing. Who would win? A fine bead of perspiration dotted her brow as she drove. She knew in her heart who was going to win, and all she could do was mark time.

Chapter Five

Although the picturesque facade of Rancho Arroyo pleased the eye, it was the *inner* working of the small complex that threatened to be the undoing of Jan Warren. The new car dealership kept reneging on delivery of the promised van, offering instead vague excuses, and the bills for the rental limousine Jan was forced to use kept mounting. The air-conditioning unit in the main lodge had to be replaced, and, to add insult to injury, the main generator gave out, and though the backup unit functioned, it failed to do the job efficiently, to the guests' acute discomfort.

The swimming pool had been inactive for three days, and the guests were becoming hostile, threatening to leave at a moments' notice. Her pleas that the filtering system was being cleaned and water pressure was low fell on unforgiving ears. All the guests cared about was the 105 degree temperature and how were they to cool off with the air-conditioning working on a hit-or-miss basis. There was no longer any cash flow and the small savings account had dwindled alarmingly. Food was being bought sparingly and paid for just as sparingly. Benjie's hospital bills were mounting faster than she could count. She was being beaten before she started. There was no way she was going to run this ranch by herself.

Jan gathered the mail and retired to her office. Slumping down in the swivel chair, she swung her booted feet on top of the desk. Lord, she was tired—more tired than when she had been holding down two jobs with a house to clean and meals to cook. It must be the heat, she told herself, plus the fact that she wasn't sleeping well.

Wearily, she massaged her temples, willing the approaching headache to evaporate. She felt like crying. No, she wanted to throw a furious tantrum. She wanted to kick and yell and scream and break things, then to cry stormily and get it all out of her system. But she couldn't do that, now that she was an adult. A pity—she would have felt so much better.

Jan pulled a piece of stationery out of her desk drawer and began to scrawl off a note to Neil. As she wrote she wondered how she could so blithely lie about how things were here at the Rancho Arroyo. Lies, all lies, she told herself. Even if she hadn't come right out and said that things were marvelous and wonderful and that she was making money hand over fist and that she was certain to make a success of the business, she had lied by omission. Consciously, she had worded her letters so they skirted the issue. She hadn't told Neil that the minibus had broken down, she had instead led him to believe that she had ordered a new minibus because there was enough capital in the ranch's account and because of a whim.

While she told him of Delilah and Gus, she had done it to describe their colorful characters. She hadn't told him that she was worried sick that her cook would stomp out and go over to the Golden Lasso and that nothing in this world—not even Gus—could bring her back again.

The taste of the glue on the back of the stamp was bitter. She applied it to the envelope and slammed her fist down on it. She'd prefer to die rather than tell Neil that she couldn't handle managing the ranch. That would be tantamount to admitting she was stupid, and she knew that Neil was not gentleman enough to refrain from saying "I told you so!"

Frowning, Jan told herself that she wasn't lying to Neil; she was merely dreaming aloud.

To Jan's weary mind and body it was inevitable that Derek Bannon should be entering her office. She didn't move but deliberately reached for a Coke bottle and took a long drink. Now what?

"I've come to make you another offer for this property," Bannon said, seating himself across the desk from Jan. His easy familiarity annoyed Jan. She took another gulp of the lukewarm soda and set the bottle down with a thump. "It's not for sale," she said curtly.

"Why?" The question sounded obscene to Jan's ears, and she momentarily saw red. How dare he come here and harass her like this? Who did he think he was?

"Because I said so. You look like a reasonably intelligent man, Mr. Bannon. Why do you refuse to accept my decision not to sell? Why are you harassing me like this? The ranch is not for sale, period."

"If you keep on like you've been going, you'll have to file for bankruptcy soon. Is that what you want? I'm willing to pay you three times what this property is worth. You're being very foolish in rejecting my generous offer."

"Why? Why are you offering me three times what the ranch is worth?" Jan asked coolly. "Nobody throws away money like that—not even rich people. Tell me why you want this ranch so badly. Your club seems to be a thriving place and equal to Las Vegas, if one is to believe my guests. What could you possibly want with this little place?"

Derek Bannon ignored the pointed question. "Shortly before your uncle's death we were in serious negotiations concerning this ranch. He agreed to sell at my price. I feel that you should honor his decision," Derek said harshly.

"I have only your word for that, Mr. Bannon. No one around here seems to know anything about your negotiations other than that you were here trying to pressure a sick old man. If I knew in my heart that what you say is true, I would sell you this ranch, but since I don't know for sure, I can't do it. My uncle had a will drawn up leaving me this property. It seems to me if he had any intention of selling Rancho Arroyo to you, he would have changed his will."

"Your uncle was not a sick old man as you imply. He was a sharp, intelligent businessman, and, let me tell you, I met my match while we were discussing terms. He knew exactly what he was doing. Why he agreed to sell I don't know. The day before he died he called me at the club and made an appointment to see me the following afternoon to finalize the deal. As you know, he died shortly after awakening."

"It's a pig in a poke, Mr. Bannon. Proof. If you can give me proof, then I'll sell—not a minute before. Now if you'll excuse me, I'm rather busy."

"I can see that you're busy," Derek Bannon said mockingly, his white teeth gleaming against his bronzed tan. "I'm giving you until August first to take advantage of my offer and after that it's withdrawn. If you file for bankruptcy, you lose everything. Think about that before you make any rash decisions," Derek said, getting up from the chair. Before she knew what he was doing, he swept her feet off the desk and stood towering over her. "Ladies," he said coldly, "never sit with their feet on a desk."

"What you mean is Andrea would never sit with her feet on a desk," Jan said spitefully. Now why had she said that? Her cheeks flushed and she was very aware of Derek's mocking eyes as he strode from her office. "I'm taking Ben back to the club with me," he called over his shoulder.

She should stop him, say something to prevent the hold he had over the boy. But how could she deprive her brother of the one main pleasure he had—seeing the Bisons work out in the field belonging to the Golden Lasso? It rankled her that Benjie had taken to the muscular man and was now calling him Derek. What did they do over there for hours on end? She admitted that she was jealous of the man's attention to her little brother, wishing secretly that it was herself he was courting.

Benjie arrived home shortly after four in the afternoon in the company of Dusty Baker. From her position behind the desk in the lobby Jan watched as Dusty opened the car door and pushed the wheelchair as close as possible for Benjie to maneuver. He tousled Benjie's hair and then followed him into the lodge. Jan smiled as Benjie introduced the famous ball player.

"I've heard a lot about you," Dusty said, indicating Benjie, who was grinning from ear to ear. "This," he said holding out a sealed envelope, "is your invitation to the Bisons' testimonial dinner. It's this evening at eight. Formal dress."

"I almost forgot," Jan apologized. "Thank you for reminding me."

"Don't thank me—thank Derek Bannon. He said he would have my scalp if I didn't deliver this when I brought Benjie home."

"Have you known Mr. Bannon long?" Jan asked pointedly.

"Sure have. He's a great guy. When his father died, he took over the club, and, let me tell you, he's one heck of an owner—just like his father. He never interferes with the managers, and when he does offer advice, he knows where he's coming from. This testimonial and vacation for the club is a treat for us. He picks up the tab once a year. I've gotta get back now. See you this evening. Hang tough, Benjie," he said, ruffling the little boy's hair a second time.

"I have to wear a shirt and tie—Andrea said so," Benjie said happily. "What are you going to wear?"

"Didn't Andrea tell you what I should wear?" Jan snapped irritably.

"No. Was she supposed to? She's wearing a dress that doesn't have straps and has a slit up the side. I saw her show it to Derek and he said it was...it was...sen...sensational. Do you have something that's sensational?"

"I'm afraid not, Benjie. There hasn't been much money lately to buy sensational clothes."

"That's what I told Derek," Benjie said off-handedly, maneuvering the chair through the lobby. "I'm going out to see how the work on the pool is coming."

Sensational, huh? Jan muttered as she ripped open the invitation. Hmm. According to the invitation, she and Benjie were to sit with Derek at his table. There was no mention of Gus or Andy, and yet Benjie was given four tickets. It made no difference, since neither Andy nor Gus expressed a desire to attend the festivities. She and Benjie would have to wing it on their own. At that moment she would have sold her soul to have a gorgeous dress to wear for the evening's entertainment. It was a night out—her first real one in over two years. It would be whatever she made it, good or bad. Clothes didn't necessarily make the person, but they sure helped.

How was she going to sit at a table with Derek Bannon and not show how uncomfortable he made her. She would blush like a schoolgirl every time she remembered how he held her, crushing his lips to hers. That heady, wonderful experience had made her aware that she was alive and that her adrenaline flowed like everyone else's. How? She just might be able to carry it off if Benjie chattered away all night long. A twenty-one-year-old woman depending on a nine-year-old to carry off an evening. It was a disgusting thing to want or even expect. "Well, Mr. Bannon, what you see is what you get," she muttered to the empty room. Hair! She had to do something about her hair, she thought wildly.

Jan checked the kitchen to be sure Delilah had everything under control. From there she checked out the work going on poolside and was reassured that by nightfall the filtering system would once again be operational and the pool ready for use by morning. She stood watching Gus give a group of youngsters a lesson in using a lasso. She whirled around in time to see a rather matronly-looking woman slide off a horse into Andy's outstretched arms. For the moment everything was under control.

A long, luxurious bubble bath later, Jan stepped from the tub and wrapped herself in a bright lemon bath sheet. She squinted down at her feet and decided not only on a manicure but a pedicure as well. The creamy mulberry nail lacquer went on smoothly, pleasing the excited girl. She had to look her best in case she found herself next to the ravishing Andrea in her sensational dress. How could she ever hope to compare to someone as gorgeous as Andrea? "I can't," Jan said dejectedly, sitting down on the edge of the tub while she fanned her nails in the air.

Her nails dry, Jan went through her closet slowly and methodically, searching for something to wear. There wasn't a lot to choose from. When she had bought clothes in the past, she had bypassed all the frivolous evening wear in favor of tailored suits and dresses she could wear to work or, if the occasion warranted, dress up with a colorful scarf or belt. There were two long dresses that were on the serviceable if not outdated list. Thoughtfully, Jan pulled a black sheath with a high mandarin collar from the hanger. It was too plain and there was nothing to dress it up with. Certainly a belt would add nothing and the high collar couldn't take a scarf. She shrugged and slipped into the dress and stood staring at her reflection. Maybe when she had her makeup on it would look better. Before she could change her mind she reached down and ripped the side seam of the gown to above the knee. A little flash of leg never hurt anyone. She had good legs—why not show them? Quickly, she threaded a needle and stitched up the seams so the frayed edges wouldn't show. Again she walked to the mirror and moved this way and that. It still needed something. Whatever it was, she didn't have it, so she would have to be content with the dress the way it was.

Jan slid her feet into wispy black sandals with spiked heels and immediately felt dressed. She toiled painstakingly over her makeup, diligently trying to cover the freckles across the bridge of her nose. Her attempt was less than successful. Well, she had tried—what more could she do? Derek Bannon probably wouldn't even notice her—especially with Andrea around.

Jan transferred the contents of her shoulder bag into a slim black envelope of a purse and left the room to wait in the lobby for Benjie. She hoped Gus had made him clean his ears. How good it was to see Gus take over the personal care of the little boy. Derek Bannon was right again. Benjie seemed to be thriving with all the male attention he was getting—especially from Gus.

Jan whistled playfully when Gus pushed the chair into the lobby. Benjie grinned. "You look...

sensational, doesn't she, Gus?" The old Indian
grinned and nodded, showing strong white teeth.
Delilah took that moment to pass through the lobby
and inspect them.

"You need something," she said, tilting her head
to the side like a bright, precocious squirrel. "You
wait, I get." She was back moments later with a
heavy silver and turquoise pendant. "White Ante-
lope, Gus's great-grandfather give to him. Is made
for woman of beauty." Before Jan could say a
word, Delilah had the heavy silver chain around her
neck. Gus nodded his approval while Delilah
beamed her pleasure.

"It's gorgeous, Delilah, and just what the dress
needed. Now I feel dressed."

Delilah laughed. "Is good—you make Mr. Bannon itch much. But," she said, wagging a plump
finger in the air, "you no let him scratch. You understand what I say."

"I understand, Delilah." Jan laughed. "Gus,
you are driving us in the rented limo, aren't you? If
we show up in the pickup, I'm afraid we'll be shown
the back door. Gus certainly isn't big on words, is
he?" Jan whispered over her shoulder to Delilah.

"Not many words, no. He do other things
good," Delilah said, closing the lobby doors behind them.

Aside from the day she had flown down the road
and circled back around to the Golden Lasso's

kitchens to retrieve Delilah, Jan had never really seen Derek's glittering establishment. She'd heard reports of its elegance from the guests staying at the Rancho who had gone for dinner at the Lasso, but nothing anyone said prepared her for what she found.

Even the tarmac in the parking lot glittered with iridescent chips of vermiculite and that twinkled under the old-fashioned lamps like stars. There was a flavor of the Old West that was defined in the lighting and split-rail fences that were painted white. It was almost like taking a step backward into the past, but instead of wagon wheels, old ox harnesses, and bleached bone steers' skulls that one expected to find, the Golden Lasso had such ornate and antique decorations that would have been quite at home even in the sophisticated society of a city like San Francisco. There was nothing of the Old Frontier here. Instead, it was a shrine to the Victorian era, complete with gaslights and over-embellished furnishings of dark mahogany and trappings of rich turkey red. While the decor could have easily become overdone and gauche, it was a marvel of good taste.

The floor of the main dining hall, except for the dance area, was carpeted in thick, Oriental-style carpeting of reds and blacks and golds. The tables were covered with lace cloths and the chairs were upholstered in a dark red tapestry. Mirrors—hundreds of them, all framed in gilt—reflected the massive chandelier hung in the center of the room, and its crystal lights danced over the silver bowls filled with roses.

Benjie seemed oblivious to all this elegance, and Jan supposed it was because of his frequent visits. She noticed that the main dining hall opened onto several small rooms, all decorated on the theme of the elegant Pullman cars that had carried passengers from the East into the world of the New Frontier. Each room was narrow, and the tables nestled against the walls, which were hung with rich brocades. Even the lights hung along the walls were gimbaled, making one almost think they could swing gently with the rocking of the train. The ceilings were paneled in gleaming dark wood, and at the far end of each "dining car" was a glass and mirrored bar.

"This is really something, Benjie." Jan let out her breath in a silent whistle.

"Yeah. Didn't I tell you?"

"No, as a matter of fact, you didn't." Jan frowned, wondering what else Benjie had failed to mention.

"Well, if you think this is something, you should see Derek's apartment. Wow!"

"I didn't know you'd been to Derek's apartment. I thought you just came here to watch the Bisons practice on the back field."

"Yeah, I do that too. But the day Derek wanted me to meet Andrea he took me into their apartment. I got to really look around because Andrea was in the shower and we had to wait for her," Benjie said with all the innocence of a nine-year-old.

Jan looked at Benjie sharply. He had said "their apartment" and that Andrea was taking a shower. The statement seemed to throw her off balance. In spite of the fact that Derek and Andrea were engaged to be married, she hadn't thought of them as living together. This new realization struck a nerve in Jan, and she felt herself blushing. Derek and Andrea could do whatever they wanted and it didn't mean anything to her, but when she thought of his arms around her and his mouth on hers, she died a little inside. What a fool she was, and what a bounder Derek was. He had committed himself totally to Andrea, and yet he wanted to play his little games with Jan. Fool, fool, she cursed herself. And you let him do it, and, more to your stupidity, you loved it.

"Hey, Dusty!" Benjie called to the tall, well-built man across the room who was motioning for them to join him at his table. "Come on, Jan. There's Dusty. We're going to be sitting with him at Derek's table."

Jan's feet moved like lead weights across the floor. The last thing in this world she wanted was to be here, in the Golden Lasso, about to sit down to a night's celebration with Derek Bannon and Andrea. Benjie maneuvered his chair over to the table where Dusty Baker waited and pulled up to the space where a place had been set minus a chair.

"Hi, remember me? I'm Dusty Baker." He extended a beefy hand that swallowed Jan's. "As I said earlier, I've heard a lot about you, Miss Warren, and all of it's good. Ben knows how lucky he is to have you for a sister. Isn't that right, Ben?" He smiled affectionately at the boy.

"You bet, Dusty. Where's Derek?"

"Oh, he's seeing to some last-minute details. It's still early—he and Andrea will be here soon." Dusty held a chair and waited for Jan to seat herself. Then he walked around to the other side of the table and sat down.

"Is this your first visit to the Golden Lasso, Miss Warren?" Dusty asked as he stirred the ice in his glass.

"Please call me Jan. And yes—I've never been here before. It's really something."

"It sure is. Andrea had a lot to do with it. She's an interior decorator, and she's outdone herself with the Lasso. It's been covered in quite a number of magazines, but I don't suppose you're the kind of girl who reads those kinds of books."

Jan blushed. It was obvious that the kind of magazines he was referring to were the girlie magazines that depicted nude women. Also, there was something about the way he mentioned Andrea. With a kind of proprietorial pride that denoted something more than a casual friendship. Dusty turned to motion to the waiter and Jan suddenly recognized his broad shoulders and the set of his head and immediately knew that Dusty Baker was the man on the plane who had joked and quipped with Andrea and made a date for a drink. As much as Jan was inclined to like the football player, she wondered what kind of man would try to make a date with his friend's fiancée. What kind of people were these who had no respect for friendship and loyalty and faithfulness? Even Derek—about to be married to Andrea—had made advances in Jan's direction. And gullible little fool that she was, she had allowed it.

Dusty ordered a drink for Jan and turned his attention back to Benjie, who preened with delight. Jan decided that whatever else she thought about these people, they certainly were kind to Ben, and that should redeem them at least a little bit.

The dining room began to fill and every so often Benjie would wave across the room at another of the Bisons. As he did, Dusty told Jan their names. Many of the players were accompanied by their wives and children, and Jan saw that many of the boys around Benjie's age waved their greetings.

"Pretty soon Ben will be out there with the other kids, running and swimming, won't you Ben?" Dusty asked.

"You betcha! Dr. Rossi says I'm coming along real fine. Isn't that right, Jan?"

"That's what the word is, Benjie. But there's still a lot of hard work ahead of you." Dusty turned to greet someone, and Benjie pulled on Jan's hand, making her lean over to hear him whisper.

"Jan, just for tonight, couldn't you call me Ben? I don't want everybody to think I'm still a baby."

Jan was almost speechless. Derek Bannon's influence over her brother was becoming insufferable. But when she looked into Benjie's eyes, she saw that this was very important to him. "All right, Ben," she whispered in return, "but I'm warning you—every time I have you alone, I'll still call you Benjie."

"Aw, Jan, that's okay for when we're alone. But not when there's somebody around, okay?" he pleaded.

"Okay," she assured him, "but don't blame me if I forget once in a while. You've been my little brother Benjie for a lot of years."

Dusty Baker rose to his feet and turned toward the entrance to the dining room. Andrea walked across the room, and, just as Benjie had predicted, her dress was sensational. A long, sleek, shimmering red that was slit from the hem practically up to her waist. It outlined every curve and line of her body, and the strapless bodice accented the smooth, flawless skin on her shoulders. The only jewelry Andrea wore was long, dangling earrings, which Jan supposed were real diamonds. Everything else about Andrea appeared to be real—why not her jewelry? Jan sighed to herself.

"Ms. Warren, this is Andrea..."

"We've met," Jan interjected hastily. She couldn't bear to hear Dusty Baker say "Derek's fiancée."

Feeling awkward and out of date in her black sheath gown, Jan accepted Andrea's welcome through stiff lips. Although Andrea's attitude seemed friendly enough, Jan couldn't seem to bring herself past the green-eyed monster to accept Andrea as a friend.

"Can you sit down with us now, honey?" Jan heard Dusty say to Andrea, and immediately she bristled at the familiarity of his tone and the pet name he used.

"I think I've done everything that needed doing." Andrea sighed wearily. "These affairs take more out of me than you could know, Dusty. Derek is settling some disagreement in the kitchen. He'll join us shortly. That is, if the chef doesn't quit and he has to broil the steaks himself." Andrea laughed, Jan supposed, at the vision of Derek, complete in chef's hat, bustling about the kitchen.

Jan saw the way the girl touched the sleeve of Dusty's jacket and the way her fingers lingered there just a little too long. There was definitely more to this relationship than met the eye.

Andrea began talking to Benjie and offered him the dish of celery sticks and olives that the waiter had deposited on their table. Jan was suddenly jealous of the easy repartee Andrea had with Benjie, and she even thought she saw Benjie blush under the lovely girl's attentions.

"You know, I've always wanted a little brother," Andrea told Benjie. "Big brothers can sometimes be a pain in the neck. They're always telling you what you can and can't do and when to do it."

Benjie laughed. "Jan's not like that—she's the best sister a guy could have. She lets me by my own man, don't you, Jan?"

Looking at Benjie with a wide-eyed amazement, Jan managed to force a smile. His own man indeed!

Jan reached for a large black olive and clumsily dropped it onto the table and watched as it rolled across the cloth onto her lap. "Lose something, Miss Warren?" Derek had come upon her so unexpectedly that Jan nearly toppled her drink.

Muttering some inane remark, Jan found the olive in the folds of her skirt and dropped it into the ashtray. She knew her face was red and that her hand trembled when she picked up her glass.

"I'm glad you brought Ben tonight," Derek said conversationally.

Jan nodded. He was glad she brought Ben—not he was glad *she* had come. As Derek moved to take the chair beside her, Jan concentrated on sipping her drink. At all costs she wanted to disguise the fact that every fiber of her being was totally conscious of his presence. She picked up the faint aroma of his after-shave and the sleeve of his tuxedo jacket brushed her shoulder as he sat down. She saw his hand, sun bronzed and masculine, against the white lace of the tablecloth. Her emotions rushed away with her, and once again she was alone with him on the desert and those capable-looking hands were in her hair and on her back, holding her close, pressing her against his magnificent length. The scent of his after-shave came to her on a wave of remembered desire as it filled her senses and she remembered the taste of his lips on hers. Stop it! her mind screamed. You can't do this to yourself! There he is, right now, this minute, joking with the girl he's going to marry. But if he really loved Andrea, her heart whispered, would he have kissed you that way?

Before she was faced with answering her own question, soft music began playing from the violin of the strolling musician and the waiters were carrying in the trays of shrimp cocktail, which signaled the beginning of the meal.

Dinner was excellent and the table conversation exceedingly pleasant. In spite of herself, Jan relaxed and found she was enjoying every minute of the evening. Benjie—or Ben, as he now preferred to be called in public—was on his best behavior, and Jan was proud that she had instilled in the boy a good amount of table manners. Derek, especially, was particularly attentive to Benjie and herself, and no mention was made of his offer to buy the Rancho, for which Jan was grateful. Even Andrea was gracious and didn't seem to mind the attention Derek was paying to Benjie and herself. But when Jan dropped her napkin and bent to retrieve it, she understood why. Beneath the cover of the lacy cloth, Dusty and Andrea were holding hands! Right there under Derek's eyes! Practically.

After her discovery of Andrea's fickleness, Jan found it increasingly difficult to be more than barely polite. After several tries, Andrea ignored Jan altogether, behaving as though she wasn't even there. It was to the men at the table that Andrea directed her attentions, and it wasn't long before all three of them, Benjie included, were eating right out of her hand.

After dinner the Bison players assembled at the long table at the head of the room, where a podium and microphones were already set up. The testimonials were gracious and even amusing, and Benjie listened and applauded and laughed at inside jokes that Jan couldn't begin to fathom. But Benjie was enjoying himself and that was all that mattered.

When Dusty Baker stepped up to the podium to receive his award, Andrea clapped long and hard. Stealing a glance at Derek, Jan noticed that he didn't seem to mind at all that his fiancée seemed to be the man's biggest fan. Finally, unable to bear another moment of the duplicity of Derek and Andrea, she asked to be excused for a breath of fresh air. Without waiting for an answer from either Derek or Andrea, Jan stood from the table and walked across the crowded room to the doors she knew led to the garden. As she left, she was aware of Derek's glance piercing her back.

Like the parking lot, the garden was lit by tall, romantic gaslights, illuminating the paths and shrubbery in a warm, yellow glow. Shadows were accentuated and the pathways shimmered with metallic chips. Everything about Derek's Lasso was indeed golden.

At a sound behind her, Jan turned on her heel and for some reason wasn't surprised to see that Derek had followed her.

"Must you always come creeping up on me?" she demanded.

"Must you always walk around in a daze, Jan?" he replied.

"Lately, it seems as though every time I turn around, there you are," she said hotly. "Why don't you go back inside and join Andrea? She must be wondering where you've gone."

"Andrea can take care of herself. Besides, she has Dusty for company, not to mention Ben." His tone was offhanded and his mouth twisted into a wry smile.

What kind of man was he? How could he speak so offhandedly about Andrea being with Dusty Baker, and what was he doing out here in the garden with her. If he cared so little about the girl he was engaged to marry, Jan knew that he would care even less for her. She straightened her back and squared her shoulders.

"I came out here to get away from the crowd and for a breath of fresh air. And you, Mr. Bannon, are creating a crowd out here in the garden, and whenever you're around I find that the air is anything but fresh." Her tone was haughty, her eyes cold and disapproving, but it seemed that nothing she could say would daunt Mr. Derek Bannon.

Derek's eyes narrowed, and in one step he was against her, holding her fast to his lean, hard body. His lips were hot and wine scented as they pressed against hers. She could feel her lips part beneath his as she struggled to free herself, as though fighting for her life. Derek held her closer, enveloping her within the strong fold of his arms.

Weakened by conflicting emotions, Jan ceased her struggles. Derek's answer was a renewed ardor as he held her and pressed long, passionate kisses to her mouth. She felt his hands on her hair, on her breasts, on the small of her back, and reaching lower.

Resistance lost, she felt herself melt into him as though becoming a part of him. Her arms reached around his neck, her mouth was pliant and yielding to his. A spectrum of newfound desires coursed through her body as she clung to him, offering herself to his caresses, submitting herself to his demands.

Suddenly, violently, she fought his advances. What was wrong with her, submitting to Derek Bannon this way? If *he* couldn't remember that he was engaged to Andrea, *she* could!

Jan lashed out blindly, her hands beating at his broad chest and reaching for his mocking face. Fury inflamed her cheeks and shame and humiliation at what she had allowed to happen brought hot tears to her eyes.

"You devil!" she shouted. "Keep your hands off me!" She lashed out again, aiming for the cold blue eyes that seemed to burn through her, turning her veins to ice.

Derek sidestepped her flailing arm, caught it by the wrist, and pulled her against him, holding her there in his iron grip.

All the weariness of the past weeks overcame her. Dry, wracking sobs of frustration caught in her throat. She was the vanquished, he the victor. Let him do with her what he would, then just leave her alone to crawl somewhere to hide.

Closely pressed against her, he held her; Jan's lips were burning from his kisses and an involuntary trembling took hold of her. Through their light clothing, she could feel the massive muscular strength of him as he molded her body to his.

Feeling his lips part from her, Jan opened her eyes and could read the desire in his. His caresses became more intimate, and again Jan surrendered herself as though all her energy was anticipating a most unexpected pleasure.

Abruptly, he pushed her away from him with such a force her teeth rattled. His eyes avoided hers; the pain of rejection pricked her eyelids. In a gruff voice he commanded, "Go home, Jan." Silently, he turned and stalked away from her.

Humiliation swallowed her and a bitterness rose to her throat. He had used her, and she, heaven help her, had helped him—enjoyed it, loved it! And now he was through with her as though she were a cast-off shoe.

Oh, how I hate him! she cried silently. I hate him! But, realizing the truth for what it was, she sobbed, "Heaven help me, I love him. I love him!"

Chapter Six

Jan refused to glance in the mirror the morning after the testimonial dinner for the Bisons. How could she have made such a fool of herself? How could she have allowed herself to be drawn into Derek Bannon's arms and enjoy it? Gus must have thought her a raving idiot when she had run across the parking lot to where he waited in the rented limo and tearfully choked out the order to get Benjie out of the dining room; they were going home!

Why did Derek Bannon have this invisible hold over her? What was there about the man that made her heart pound and her senses reel? She had been in the presence of other men who were almost as handsome as Derek. Good looks and fancy clothes didn't account for the way he made her feel. She thought to herself, I can't be in love with him! I don't want to be in love with him! "I can't handle this," she cried in a broken voice. I have to see to Benjie and the Rancho, and I don't need all this emotional turmoil in my life—especially not now.

She looked around the room wildly, as though hoping some answer was going to leap out from the four walls and make everything all right. It was a new day; she had to get on with everyday living and not think about Derek Bannon and how he made her feel. It was an impossible order, and she recognized it for what it was. She could no more stop thinking about Derek than she could stop breathing.

He had given her till August 1 to decide about selling Rancho Arroyo. He was right about one thing; it would be better to sell the ranch than to file for bankruptcy and lose everything. And that was where she was headed eventually. The bills would mount and the ranch would be sold to cover the bills. And one thing was certain—on the open market, with her back to the wall, she wouldn't get half what Derek was offering for the ranch.

If she sold the ranch now, she could bank the money for Benjie's education and go back to New York to the big old house. Big old house. Maybe the bank would give her a loan if she put up the house as collateral. Aha! Derek Bannon didn't know about the house back east. How long did it take to get a loan? If she went to the bank today, she could at least set the wheels in motion. All the papers from her parents' estate were in a manila envelope in the office safe. She would take everything with her and hope the bank would realize what a valuable property she held title to. If it took only two or three weeks, she felt confident that she could stall off the creditors for at least that long. However, she thought morbidly, perhaps that would be a mistake. If guests kept canceling their reservations and moving over to the Golden Lasso, she would be pouring money down the drain.

If there was only someone to talk to, to go to for advice, to confide in. There was no one. She had only herself to depend on. Perhaps the banker would help her. If she was lucky, the loan officer might be able to advise her.

Three hours later, Jan exited the bank feeling more morose than when she had entered. While friendly and helpful, the loan officer had not been overenthusiastic about making her a loan. He used words like sizeable and pointed out that she was a novice to this sort of business and that there was the competition of the Golden Lasso to consider. His voice had dropped a degree when he said that appraisal took several weeks and one simply did not hurry a bank. Everything in good time. He would call, he told Jan, when he saw tears trickle down her cheeks. "If he had just patted me on the head, I would have felt better," Jan mumbled as she hailed a cab to take her out to the medical center.

Dr. Rossi's youth and exuberance were evident when he told her of the progress Benjie was making in his physical therapy. "Dusty Baker and Derek Bannon have had a great deal to do with that progress. You have those men to thank for Ben's positive attitude, Miss Warren. And, of course, your own patience and work in helping Ben perform his daily exercises."

Jan bristled. If there was one thing she didn't need right now, it was another Derek Bannon fan.

"Ben thinks a great deal of Derek," Dr. Rossi went on to say. "With his encouragement, I predict that Ben will be walking very soon."

"Dr. Rossi, I'm so happy! That's fantastic news! I'm so grateful. I had no idea things would progress so quickly." Jan smiled. Benjie's happiness depended upon his walking again, and anything that made Benjie happy was good for her, too.

"A positive attitude and hope are something we here at the medical center never discount. As a matter of fact, we depend on them. I just wish all our patients responded as well as Ben."

Outside his office Dr. Rossi's receptionist told Jan that the billing office would like her to stop by and see them. Jan smiled nervously and stepped out into the corridor. She didn't know if she was happy or sad. Certainly happy that Benjie was doing so remarkably well, but sad that she had to see about paying the bill. Would they refuse to treat Benjie once they discovered that she couldn't meet the full responsibility of the bill? There was no decision to be made. If it came down to Benjie, she would sell the Rancho to Derek Bannon if the bank refused to give her a loan. She wouldn't lose sight of the fact that Benjie came first.

Surprisingly, the woman who was in charge of the billing office understood her problem and worked on it accordingly. "It's not the center's policy to deny help to those who can't afford to pay. We have a very wealthy patron here in Phoenix who donates often and handsomely. You can pay when you're able, Miss Warren. Just fill out this pledge form. Actually—" the woman smiled "— it's not even a pledge. Mr. Bannon said it was important for people to feel that they weren't charity cases. And do you know, he's right?" the woman beamed. "Even several years after treatment, many of our patients continue to pay on their bills. Even if it's small amounts at first. So everyone benefits from Derek Bannon's generosity—the clinic and the new patients."

Jan left the credit office in a daze. Derek Bannon certainly was an enigma. No two people saw him in the same light. How could a kind, wonderful, generous person as the woman in the credit office described set out to ruin a poor girl from New York who only wanted to set the Rancho on a paying basis to support her brother and herself? And how could such a philanthropic, humane man stand in the wings like a vulture waiting for her to go bankrupt so he could snatch up her property?

A quick glance at her watch told her it was almost noon and time for lunch. She looked around for a suitable restaurant, but the only thing in sight was a cocktail lounge that had a sign proclaiming they served businessmen lunches. Why not? The next bus back to the ranch wouldn't leave till two fifteen, so she had plenty of time. Jan decided to treat herself.

"A vodka and tonic. And I think I'll have a Waldorf salad," she said bravely to the waitress. She hated eating alone, and when the occasion came up, she never ordered a drink, thinking all eyes were on a solitary woman eating and drinking by herself. For the moment she felt the need of the artificial stimulation to get her mind in gear again. Why did Derek Bannon always toss her a curve? Just when she thought she had him figured out, he did something to confuse her and make himself look like the proverbial knight in shining armor.

"Drinking alone, Miss Warren?" a cool voice demanded. Jan almost choked on the liquid in her mouth. Maybe if she ignored him he would go away. But men like Derek Bannon never went away. It was impossible to ignore such a masculine presence. Setting her glass down with expert precision, she stared at the man who was seating himself opposite her.

"Permit me to recommend the baked sole." Jan said nothing. "Have you given my offer any more thought?" Derek Bannon asked quietly.

"Yes." She deliberately avoided saying more.

"What's your decision?"

"I haven't decided. You said August first. I'll give you my decision then." Their eyes locked, and it was Jan who flushed and lowered her gaze, remembering how his eyes had softened as he stared into hers right before she melted into his arms. Was he remembering, too?

"I meant it when I said I would withdraw the offer at that time," Derek said coolly.

"I'm sure you did. Your offer was more than generous. Why can't you understand how important it is for me to keep the ranch? I have to try to make a go of it. You can't possibly need it. You appear to be very wealthy, and your club must be making you a handsome profit. My ranch isn't an eyesore that would offend your guests, so if you would level with me, I might be more amenable to your request. Wanting something just for the sake of wanting it is not reason enough. You might have been born with a silver spoon but I wasn't. I've

worked since I was sixteen, and for the past two
years I've held down two jobs, seven days a week,
to be sure Benjie got the best I could give him. This,
Mr. Bannon, is my best, and I can't let you take it
from us. No, that's not right—I *won't* let you take
it from us. If you'll excuse me, I have to get back to
the bus station."

Derek Bannon stared at the tight-lipped girl who
was sliding out of the booth. "I'm going back to
the Lasso. If you want a ride, you're welcome to
come with me." Jan ignored him as she laid some
bills on the table and paid for her uneaten meal.
There was no way she could handle the ride back to
the ranch sitting next to Derek Bannon. Right now
it was all she could do to hold the threatening tears
in check. She was through the revolving door and
hailing a cab before Derek could get out of the
booth. "And I'll bet that's the first time one of
your women ever refused you anything," she muttered to herself.

Jan's bus was already boarding when she climbed
from the cab. Derek Bannon wheeled his sports car
in front of the bus and came to a screeching halt.
Jan didn't look in his direction but immediately
took her place in line.

"This is ridiculous. I'm going right by the ranch.
If you take this bus, you have to walk from the
highway to Rancho Arroyo. Stop being so silly and
come with me," Derek said, taking her posses-

sively by the arm. Jan pulled away, his touch, like a firebrand, scalding her bare arm.

"I'm taking this bus. I came on the bus and I'm going home on the bus. It's not my fault that you don't understand the word no. No, Mr. Bannon, I do not want a ride home. And," she said tartly, "you can just come by the Rancho and pick up that cat you had the gall to send me."

"Is this man bothering you, Miss?" the bus driver demanded gruffly.

"He certainly is. He tried to pick me up in a coc...restaurant."

"Beat it, buddy, and leave the young ladies alone or I'll have to call a policeman. You good-looking playboys are all alike. You see a pretty face and you think all you have to do is move in. Take that fancy rig of yours out of here right now so I can get this bus moving."

Jan was delighted at the look of acute discomfort on Derek's face. Two put-downs in the space of five minutes. She smiled winningly and waved a jaunty salute. She shuddered at Derek's cold, unreadable face. He looked as though he wanted to murder someone. Serves him right, Jan thought as she leaned back in her seat.

When Jan left the bus on the highway, she almost expected to see Derek waiting for her, and she was disappointed that he wasn't. The heat was unbearable and before she was halfway home she wished she had accepted his offer. Her sandal straps were rubbing, and she knew she would have king-size blisters the moment she removed her shoes. She could feel her makeup run, and she knew her hair was wet and tangled, hanging limply to her head. She didn't know when she had ever felt so miserable.

When Jan hobbled up the flagstone walkway leading to the kitchen, she thought she was going to faint. Delilah clucked over her like a mother hen, bathing her face in cool water and then wrapping her blistered feet in an herb-scented cloth. A frosty glass of lemonade was placed in her hand to be refilled twice. "Where's that weird cat that came in the mail?" Jan demanded petulantly.

"Not one cat anymore. Nine cats now," Delilah said, pointing to a spot near the open-hearth fireplace in the gigantic kitchen.

"Remarkable," Jan said through clenched teeth. "He's sadistic, Delilah. Do you have any idea how much it's going to cost to feed nine cats?" Delilah shook her head mournfully. "A lot, a fortune. I can't afford it. Tomorrow I'm mailing them back to him C.O.D."

"You much mad at Mr. Bannon?" Delilah inquired, a frown on her face. "You much mad because he kiss you or because he no kiss you? He kiss good, no?"

"He kiss good, yes," Jan giggled. "Too good."

Delilah waddled over to the stove. "Much good kiss, so you send back cats. Not good sense," she muttered as she stirred a bubbling pot on the stove.

Chapter Seven

As always, after being in Derek Bannon's company, Jan felt inadequate. This was the third time he had reduced her to a mass of silly putty. She must be doing something wrong. It wasn't her fault she didn't know how to act around people like Derek and the beautiful Andrea. She admitted that she hated the word *homespun,* but that's exactly what she was—a down-home country girl. And while she hadn't just dropped off the watermelon truck, she was incapable of playing in Derek Bannon's league.

And on top of that was the niggling suspicion of why Bannon wanted her property. What possible use could he make of it? Why wouldn't he say why he wanted it?

Somehow Jan managed to work her way through the day without any mishaps of any kind. Things were running smoothly for a change and she wanted to enjoy the calm atmosphere, if not to revel in it. Derek Bannon was the stuff dreams were made of and that's where she would relegate him in her mind. She would allow herself the luxury of thinking of him only when she drifted off to sleep. If she allowed him to get under her skin, she couldn't function. Delilah was right—he made her itch.

The day's work behind her, Jan watered the tubs of flowers around the pool and then sat down to relax with a cold glass of ginger ale. She felt good, knowing she had worked a full day and somehow managed to cope and make everyone happy. She deserved this brief respite before putting Benjie to bed.

Delilah seemed always to be the bearer of bad tidings, and this time was no different. Jan watched her approach the pool area, her bright eyes searching out Jan in the dim lantern light. "Bad news," she said matter of factly. "Andy break leg here, here and here. Three places," she said, holding up three plump fingers. "I call ambulance."

"What?" Jan exclaimed, jumping up from the chaise longue. "How ... never mind." If there was one thing she didn't need, it was one of Delilah's explanations. "Where is he?"

"On floor in bunkhouse. He dreaming and fall out. Simple."

Jan was sure Delilah was right. Anything more would have been too confusing. Now what was she going to do?

"Andy, are you all right?" she asked, bending over the lanky man.

"Yeah, I'm okay, but the leg is busted in three places—at least, that's what Delilah said. I'm embarrassed," he said, gritting his teeth in pain. "I don't know how it happened. One minute I was asleep dreaming about all those lovelies over at the Golden Lasso and *wham,* I was falling out of the bunk. I tried to grab the rail and that's all I remember."

"Delilah called for the ambulance; it's on the way. Here, let me put a pillow under your head. Do you want me to have Gus ride along with you to the hospital?"

"I'd appreciate that, Jan. Listen, do you think you could do me a favor and not...what I mean is, people might think..."

Jan grinned. "I'll tell them you did it in the line of duty. Don't worry about it. Do you think some brandy might ease the pain? I'm afraid to give you anything else."

"I get," Delilah said, waddling off to fetch the brandy.

"Did Delilah check your leg?"

"Are you kidding? She just looked at it and then went, '*Tsk, tsk, tsk,* is broke, three places.' When she says something, you can count on it."

"Amazing," Jan said, shaking her head.

"That she is. Your uncle regarded her as a real treasure."

The brandy arrived at the same time the ambulance did. The attendants vetoed the brandy, to Delilah's annoyance. She fixed her shoe-button eyes on the youngest attendant and said, "You stupid—brandy make him sweat. Where you learn medicine, Sears Roebuck? *Tsk, tsk, tsk,*" she muttered as she downed the fiery liquid and waddled back to the kitchen.

The young attendant looked at Jan and shook his head. "His leg is broken in three places—please be careful," Jan pleaded.

"How do you know his leg is broken in three places?" the older man asked.

"I just know." Not for the world would she admit that she was taking Delilah's word for the three breaks in Andy's leg.

Andy winked at her; he wasn't about to tell them either. His look clearly stated, "Why shake up medical science?"

By the time she checked on Benjie and found him propped up in bed with a Hardy Boys book, she was bone tired. She felt a tug at her heart as she looked at the little boy. How game he was; he never complained and he always had a smile for her. He looked wan and tired, though.

"Benjie, how do you feel?"

"I feel tired, but it's a good tired. Dr. Rossi and Derek say so. Dr. Rossi said I was making... re... remarkable progress and Derek said he was proud of me. Dusty Baker said so, too. You shouldn't worry about me, Jan—the guys are taking good care of me. Aren't they the greatest?" he asked happily.

Jan nodded. "If they're making you happy, then, yes, they're the greatest," she said, bending over him to give him a good-night kiss. "Ten minutes and lights out. Tomorrow is another day."

"Jan, would you like to go on a picnic to Rattlesnake Canyon with me and Derek. He said it was okay if you came along as long as you brought the food."

A sharp retort rose to her lips but Jan squelched it. "I'll think about it. Remember, ten minutes. Goodnight, Benjie."

"'Night, Jan," Benjie mumbled as he joined the adventuresome Hardy Boys in one of their wild escapades.

What kind of left-handed invitation was that? You can come along if you bring the food. She dutifully answered Neil's letter, the thought of the picnic continually on her mind. *Humph,* she sniffed as she got ready for bed. She was planning the menu as she drifted off to sleep.

The digital clock on the night table read 3:18 A.M. when she heard Benjie cry out. She lay quietly, waiting to see if the sound was repeated. It had been a long time since he had had nightmares. He wasn't crying; he was groaning when she reached his room and flicked on the light switch. "What's wrong?" she asked anxiously.

"My legs. They're all cramped up," Benjie cried. "They hurt, Jan. Make it go away!"

"I'll call Dr. Rossi. Do you want me to get Gus to come and stay with you while I make the call?"

"Gus went to the hospital with Andy and they aren't back yet." Benjie groaned. "Please, Jan, do something..." His words were stopped by the effort to grit his teeth and bear the pain.

Jan ran into her room and called the hospital only to find out that Dr. Rossi had left for Tucson late that afternoon and wouldn't be back in his office until late the next day. Since it was an emergency, they would try to reach him and have him call her back.

"Jan, get Derek. He'll know what to do," Benjie pleaded. "He stays in the therapy room while I have my treatments."

"But, Benjie, Derek isn't a doctor..."

"I want Derek," Benjie said, crying now, tears streaming down his cheeks. "Please, Jan, please get him."

"Okay, okay, honey, I'll call him. I'll be right back." Jan raced down to the first floor and pounded on Delilah's door, waking her and instructing her to go to Benjie while she made the call.

The main switchboard at the Golden Lasso answered and rang Derek Bannon's apartment suite. The line was busy. Trying to control her panic, Jan asked them to please break into the line. It was an emergency with Ben Warren down at the Rancho Arroyo. The young man at the switchboard was sympathetic and came back on the line.

"I'm terribly sorry, but the phone must be off the hook. If I can reach someone, I'll have them go over to Mr. Bannon's apartment. You do understand that I can't leave the desk."

Jan slammed down the receiver. She would have to go to the Lasso and get Derek herself. She would have to use the pickup truck; the rented limo had been returned that afternoon. Taken back, actually—she forced herself to face reality.

Jan ground the gears in the old pickup as she raced up the road. She would bring Derek Bannon back to the Rancho if she had to drag him out of bed. Benjie had said something about his private apartment being somewhere near the tennis courts.

Halfway to the Golden Lasso, the pickup coughed and sputtered, and before she had gone another five hundred feet, it died altogether. Jan shifted into neutral and turned the key. Nothing. Twice more she tried. Again nothing. Climbing out from the truck, she slammed the door shut with a vengeance. Darn old dilapidated, confounded machine! Nothing worked. Nothing!

Now what was she to do? She was already halfway to the Lasso—turning back now would be foolish. She had to go on ahead. The night was chilly, as always in the desert. Her Western boots rubbed against the unhealed blisters. She had hurriedly pulled them on but hadn't taken the time to search for socks. At that moment she would have cheerfully given her back teeth for a skateboard.

By the time she reached the cobblestoned driveway to the Golden Lasso, she was perspiring with the effort of the walk. Her hair hung in limp strands about her ashy face. Her silk pajamas, emblazoned with green turtles, was plastered to her body, and she was limping from a bruise on the bottom of her sore feet. The thin robe that matched her pajamas flapped about her like bat wings. Somewhere along the way she had lost the belt. She wanted to cry, but she couldn't afford the luxury.

Instead, she sniffed, wiped at her mouth, and headed for the rear of the Golden Lasso. If she couldn't find Derek's apartment immediately, she would scream to raise the dead. Someone would come running. She hoped.

Jan found the tennis courts and looked about for what might look like private apartments. Someone was up—there was a light in the window to the left of the courts. She squared her shoulders and marched over to the door and rapped on it sharply. Andrea, clad in a wispy affair of black lace, stood framed in the doorway, her eyebrows arched in amusement. "Jan, what are you doing here at this hour?"

Licking her lips and swallowing hard, Jan replied, "I'm looking for Derek...Mr. Bannon. Is he here? I must see him—it's very important. It's about Benjie...Ben. It's important." No one should look that beautiful at four in the morning. Jan knew she was going to cry.

Sensing her desperation, Andrea opened the door wider and ushered Jan into the living room. "I'll go get Derek; I'll be right back. Can I get you something, Jan? Water?"

Wordlessly, Jan nodded her head. Her mouth was so dry and parched, her tongue was thick and sticking to the roof of her mouth.

Andrea brought her a tall glass of iced water and said she would go get Derek. Impatiently, Jan paced the apartment, oblivious to its elegance and charm. All she knew was that Benjie was home and in pain and needed her and that she'd been gone too long already. Her pacing took her near a glass and chrome desk at the far end of the room. On the desk were blueprints, and the lettering at the bottom of the page stopped Jan in her tracks. "Rancho Arroyo—Redevelopment."

Upon closer examination, Jan discovered the prints were indeed of the ranch. There was the main lodge and along the trails the twelve cabins and swimming pool . . . Derek Bannon certainly lost no time. He was so confident that she would sell him the Rancho that he'd already consulted an architect about redeveloping the site. Reaching out to turn the page and try to discover exactly what Derek Bannon intended to do with the property *if* she should sell it to him, a voice startled her.

"Trick or treating, Miss Warren?" Derek Bannon said coolly. "To what do I owe the pleasure of this visit at—" he looked at the clock over the mantel "—four o'clock in the morning. Are those turtles?" he asked, touching the collar of the thin robe.

Jan was exasperated. "Yes, they're turtles and, no, I'm not trick or treating for Halloween. I need you to help Benjie. I don't know what to do for him and Dr. Rossi is in Tucson. Benjie has severe cramps in his legs. He's crying for you. Benjie never cries. Will you come?'' she pleaded.

"Of course, I'll come. Where's your car? I'll follow you back."

"My pickup broke down when I was halfway here. I came the rest of the way on foot. I had no other choice. Your phone is off the hook!'' she accused hotly, holding back the tears. "That's why I came in person—the switchboard couldn't get through."

Derek cast an angry glance at Andrea, who shrank from his silent accusation.

"Do you mind if I go back with you?'' she said, the tears that had been held in check now running in rivulets down her cheeks. "But first I have to take these boots off—my feet are covered in blisters."

Derek stared at her for a moment before he scooped her up in his arms and carried her to his car. "You weigh about as much as a postage stamp. Do you eat?"

"Of course I eat,'' Jan muttered as she settled herself in the bucket seat. She tugged at the leather boots and could feel the skin leave the backs of her heels. She winced and then sighed with relief. She felt Derek's eyes on her, but she refused to look at him, knowing that if she did she would cry.

The ride was mercifully short, and Derek was hardly out of his car before he asked where he could find Ben.

"He's up in his room, second floor. Delilah is with him," Jan responded, climbing out of the low sports car, her feet aching.

Benjie was rolling around in his narrow bed, groaning with pain and biting his lip against crying out. When he saw Derek, his face lit up a bit and he tried to smile.

"It looks like you're having a problem," Derek said quietly, the low sound of his voice instilling confidence in both Benjie and Jan. "Jan, run a tub. Delilah, go to my car and get the bag out of the back seat and bring it here." Both women rushed off to do his bidding while Derek pushed up the little boys pajama legs. "You're going to feel this and it's going to hurt like the devil in the beginning. Can you handle it?" he asked as his strong hands massaged the boy's thin calf muscle.

Benjie dug his elbows into the mattress and gritted his teeth. "Boy, does that ever hurt."

"I know. Take a deep breath and let it out slowly. Count backwards from one hundred and make sure you don't miss any numbers. How's the water coming?" he called out to Jan.

"It's ready," Jan called, testing the water for just the right temperature.

"Good, I'll put him in the tub, and when your cook brings my bag in, take the jar of yellow ointment and warm it in a saucepan." Derek came to the bathroom door, his blue eyes serious and his tone very low and deep. "We have a tough night ahead of us Jan. It's going to be rough for Ben. We can do it, can't we?"

Jan looked up into his eyes. Derek instilled such confidence, such a positive attitude, it was little wonder that Benjie adored him. And the way he had said "us." "We've" got a tough night ahead of "us" warmed Jan and made her feel as though she wasn't alone.

Derek went back into the bedroom for Benjie and lifted him from the bed. "Hey, Jan," he called, just as she was about to head for the kitchen, "do you think you can change your clothes? When I was Ben's age, I wasn't allowed to have a pet, a real pet. So my parents compromised and let me have a turtle. I hated that turtle. I still hate turtles."

"What happened to it?" Benjie asked inquisitively as Derek lowered him into the tub.

"You won't believe this, but that turtle lived for twenty years," Derek replied before breaking into the misadventures of himself as a young boy and his detested turtle, who seemed to have no other purpose in life except to torment the young Derek. Jan could see him bent over the tub, rubbing Benjie's thin legs. A smile played about the corners of her mouth as she reached for her jeans and a pull-over. She could change in the kitchen while the ointment was heating. She suspected she under-stood why Derek had wanted her to change out of the thin, silky, clinging pajamas.

All through the night Jan and Derek took turns massaging Benjie's legs. It was eight o'clock when Benjie was finally dressed in clean pajamas and sound asleep. Jan's arms ached as well as her head. She smiled wanly to Derek who put his arm around her shoulder.

"You did okay, Jan. Ben will be fine now. But the cramps will come again. It's part of the healing process. When they do, call me. I'll come over."

"You must be tired," Jan said. "Would you like some breakfast?"

"I thought you'd never ask. I'd like the biggest and best breakfast Delilah can dish up."

"Then that's exactly what you'll have. Let's let Delilah surprise us."

Jan enjoyed watching Derek make a path through the bacon and eggs and weave his way through a stack of blueberry pancakes. She picked at her food, exhausted by the trials of the night. And into her head popped a vision of Andrea in her wispy black nightie. "I'm sorry if I interrupted your... your morning. As I told you, your phone was off the hook."

Derek frowned. "Sometimes Andrea is very careless. It won't happen again."

Jan was silent and sipped her coffee. What had she expected him to say? Benjie had already informed her that Andrea was living with Derek.

"Has Ben asked you about the picnic in Rattlesnake Canyon?"

Jan laughed. "In a manner of speaking. He said I was invited if I brought the food."

"Well?"

Suddenly uncomfortable under his scrutiny, Jan nodded.

"Just don't make peanut butter sandwiches. I hate them. Almost as much as I hate turtles," Derek said as he strode through the lobby.

"I'll remember that," Jan said, making a mental note to burn those pajamas the first chance she got. The second thing she would do was throw out all the peanut butter and jelly in the kitchen. It was a good thing Derek Bannon hadn't told her to jump from a second story window. She must be out of her mind!

Chapter Eight

Benjie's excitement was contagious; he was excited over the promised picnic with Derek Bannon. In spite of herself and her own confusion concerning Derek, Jan found she had to smile and was actually anticipating the day just as Benjie was. There wasn't any need to fool herself about Derek any longer. The few kisses had meant nothing to him, and she had to take the cue and not allow these strange emotions he aroused in her to take such importance in her life. Derek was probably sowing the last of his wild oats before he married Andrea. If she were fool enough to let him kiss her and fool enough to suppose—no, hope—that it meant any-

thing to him, then she deserved whatever came her
way.

It had taken a great deal of reflection and hard
thinking to come to terms with how she felt about
Derek Bannon. Now, after pondering the logic of
it all, she knew that she had to accept the fact that
she meant nothing at all to him. All the emotions
were on her part. It was difficult to come to grips
with something like that, but Jan resolved that
when Derek married Andrea she wouldn't be left
with a broken heart. Whatever it took to defend
herself against the wonderful and stirring things he
did to her whenever he was near, she would do it.

Jan busied herself in Delilah's kitchen under the
little woman's watchful eye. Carefully, she packed
the picnic basket with a wide assortment of food
that had taken quite awhile for her to prepare. It
was the usual kind of picnic food that she and
Benjie always enjoyed. If it didn't meet with Derek's gourmet palate, then that was his problem. If
she had to torment herself by going on this picnic,
she was at least going to enjoy what she would eat.

A sudden disconcerting thought occurred to Jan.
What if Derek had invited Andrea to go along with
them? Jan groaned and snapped the lid of the picnic hamper closed. She could almost see the beautiful girl wrinkle her nose at the hard-boiled eggs
and paper napkins. And fried chicken! In those
perfectly manicured hands! Gracious.

What did Derek see in Andrea? It was true she was beautiful and glamorous and dressed like a fashion model, but she certainly didn't rain affection down upon Derek. And at the testimonial dinner she had actually had the gall to flirt and hold hands with Dusty Baker under the table. And what kind of friend was Dusty Baker to play around with Derek's fiancée? It was all too much. Jan decided she had heard of the jet set and that they played by a different set of rules, but she didn't have to like it and knew she could never be a part of it. Some small voice echoed: But you already are. You let Derek kiss you and stir up all those strange, yearning emotions. You're no better than Dusty Baker or Andrea or even Derek.

"Well, not any longer," Jan spoke aloud without realizing it. "Derek Bannon's kissing days are over," she said tartly, puzzling Delilah, who watched her as she marched out of the kitchen toting the heavily laden picnic basket.

"Here he comes, Jan," Benjie cried excitedly. "Right on time. Derek is right on time all the time. He says punctuality is the mark of a successful man. He's not like you, Jan. You're always late. Andrea is always late, too. Derek says she has to change her clothing six times before she makes a decision. I told Derek you don't do that, but you look in the mirror a lot, and he said, 'Same difference.'" Benjie babbled happily as Derek climbed from the car.

"Is everyone ready?" Jan strained her eyes into the bright sun to see if there were any other passengers in the high-axled four-wheel-drive station wagon. Maybe Derek got tired waiting for the sixth change and left without Andrea. Jan smiled. She would make an effort to be more punctual in the future. She lumped that thought into the same category as the turtles on her pajamas and throwing out the peanut butter and jelly. It was a stupid thought. It wouldn't make any difference what she did. Derek Bannon was getting married to someone else. And the thought was always with her that his deadline to sell the Rancho was bearing down on her with bared teeth. She felt a headache coming on and she knew that if she gave into it the day would be ruined for Benjie as well as herself. Why couldn't she just enjoy it for what it was and then forget about it? Because, she thought, as she watched Derek's broad back as he held the door for Benjie, I'm in love with him

Derek moved to the side in time to see the flush creep up her cheeks. "You better bring a hat—this sun is brutal today." Jan walked back inside on trembling legs for the worn and battered Stetson she had confiscated from her uncle's belongings. She didn't like this feeling of being out of control and at some man's whim, and that's what it was. Why couldn't he look at her the way he looked at Andrea? Why couldn't he say nice things to her the way he said them to Benjie and Andrea? Why was he always so cool and mocking when he looked at her? Why should he be anything else? He was engaged to marry Andrea. He was definitely a male chauvinist like Neil. She squared her shoulders. Today she wouldn't let him get to her. She could be just as cool and just as mocking. The only difference was she would have to work at it, whereas with Derek Bannon it was a natural trait.

"Did you forget anything?" Derek asked casually, eyeing the picnic hamper.

"Gosh, no, Derek. Jan was up before the birds packing everything." Benjie grinned from his seat in the back of the car.

"Then I guess we're ready for a day in the desert. After you, Jan," he said, holding open the door. Jan nodded coolly and slid into the deep seat. Their eyes met as Derek moved to close the door. Jan felt the familiar flush and was the first to look away.

"Aren't we taking my chair, Derek?" Benjie asked anxiously.

Derek leaned over the back of the seat. "How would you manage it in the sand? If I thought you needed it, I would have put it in the trunk. I brought along a canvas chair and that spare set of crutches you leave at the Lasso. That should do it."

"If you say so," Benjie said happily, leaning back into the seat. "I'm ready if you are."

Jan, too, leaned back, determined to enjoy the drive into the desert. Somehow she managed to keep up her end of the conversation in a limited way, always aware of Derek's nearness. Each time his hand moved to the gear shift she thought he was going to touch her leg; instead, he shifted expertly, the muscles in his thighs tightening and relaxing as he let the clutch in and out. Her heart alternated between wild flutterings and heavy pounding. What was wrong with her? He had no right, she thought angrily, to have the power to make her feel this way, especially since he was soon to be married. Surely he knew she was attracted to him. Why did he insist on being with her and using Benjie as an excuse? Or was she the one who was using Benjie as an excuse?

"Penny for your thoughts," Derek said softly.

Startled, Jan turned from viewing the roadside and stared at Derek. She smiled sadly. "They were deep, dark, and dire, and I don't think you really want to hear them. Besides, I'd never let them go for a mere penny." Derek's eyes narrowed. He reached for the polished sunglasses on the visor and slid them on with one hand.

Jan sensed, rather than saw, the tightening of his shoulders. She grimaced as she turned to viewing the Arizona landscape. Benjie was chattering away and Derek was answering him. She was safe for a while longer before she had to contribute to the conversation. She should be thinking about what she was going to do when Derek's deadline to sell or not to sell the ranch was up. If she didn't sell out to him, she could be left with a white elephant. If she did manage to hold on and try to make a go of Rancho Arroyo, how could she live down the road from Derek Bannon and his wife, Andrea? She couldn't. There was no decision to be made. She wouldn't spoil the day for Benjie. She would tell Derek later, or tomorrow. She and Benjie would live in Phoenix until he completed his treatments at the center and then they would head back for New York. With the money from the sale of the Rancho, she wouldn't have to work so many hours to make ends meet. Somehow things would work out. The decision made to sell out to Derek, she felt drained, emotionally and physically. She risked another glance at Derek. He turned, his expression behind the polished glasses unreadable. She hoped he couldn't see the tears in her eyes. Impossible dreams were just that. Impossible dreams. This was reality and she had better learn to live with it.

The four-wheel drive station wagon bounced easily on its high axles, affording an overview of the land. Neither Benjie nor Jan had come so far into the desert before, and Derek obligingly pointed out the sights. Low hills stained a dusky purple because the sun hadn't risen sufficiently to illuminate them rose in the distance. Barrel cactus raised their thorny heads out of the hard-baked earth, and Derek made them laugh when he said he could imagine the plants with huge eyes staring out of their limbless bodies and watching the world go by.

Derek seemed to be looking for something as he slowed the vehicle and pulled over to the side of the road close to an outcropping of tall, spiky cactus. There among the thorns was the most beautiful pink flower Jan had ever seen. Derek explained it was a night-blooming cactus, and because the sun hadn't reached it yet, it was still open. The delicate pink petals moved slightly in the breeze, and Jan and Benjie watched, transfixed, as the sun slowly crept among the branches of the plant and the lovely flower closed upon itself.

Derek drove slowly, pointing out ferns and the different kinds of cactus and flowering bushes, explaining that when most people thought of the desert they thought of a barren waste. Nothing could have been further from the truth, Jan thought. Here was life and harmony. The hills dipped and gave way to the roads; mesquite and tumbleweed dusted the earth, and yuccas and boulders kept a companionable silence. And above it all was the sky, scrubbed and blue and relentless. In a few short weeks she had come to love the desert even more than she had loved the green mountains of upstate New York. And when she must leave Arizona, as she knew she must, she would remember and mourn.

"We're here," Derek announced, swinging the wagon into a driveway paved with gravel and cutting the engine.

"But this...where...I thought you said we were going to have a picnic in the desert," Jan said, looking around at the small adobe house with its red tiled roof that sat back from the driveway and was surrounded by lush foliage. "Where is this place?" she demanded, sensing a trick on Derek's part.

He laughed. "This is the desert. Ben's doctor Bob Rossi's idea of the desert. He calls it his oasis. How do you like it? There's a pool in the back, complete with a Jacuzzi for Ben. That's why I wanted to come here."

"How does he keep all the plants and trees? And roses!" Jan gasped.

"He was lucky and he tapped into an underground spring. Fantastic, isn't it? I've got the keys, if you want to go inside and freshen up."

"It's breathtaking! It rivals any garden back home," Jan said, climbing from the car, forgetting about Benjie as she examined first one colorful plant and then another. "And there's moss—I don't believe it!" she laughed, bending down to feel the velvety softness at her feet. "It's almost like back home with the trees and the roses! I can't believe the roses!"

"The place is for sale," Derek said quietly. "Bob Rossi is moving back to Rhode Island in October to open a clinic." Jan was too busy poking beneath the shrubbery to hear his words and missed Derek's sly wink in Benjie's direction.

The place was perfect and incredibly beautiful. Here was the majesty of the desert and the nostalgia of home. Here was the perfect blending of two opposite worlds, and she knew, without fail, that here she could be happy for the rest of her life.

"Where are we going to have the picnic? Are you going to carry Benjie? We should have brought his chair," she accused. "He could get around here," Jan said, motioning to the paved walkways.

Derek grinned and whistled sharply. A young boy of perhaps seventeen came around the side of the house leading a pony and cart. "Now if you had a choice, which would you prefer? A wheelchair or one of these?" Derek said, pointing at the pony cart.

"Oh, wow!" Benjie exclaimed as he peered out the car window. "Do I really get to ride in that?"

"All day, if you want. There's lots for you to explore. Nick will ride along with you on horseback to keep an eye on you. He'll be perfectly safe," Derek said sharply to Jan, who was about to protest.

Jan snapped her mouth shut and fumed. She hadn't been about to protest over Benjie's safety, but because it appeared that she was about to be left alone with Derek.

Nick lifted Benjie from the car and settled him comfortably in the pony cart. He handed the excited boy the reins and grinned down from his perch atop a tall roan horse. "The pony's name is Sally, and she works at two speeds. Slow and stop. Just hold the reins loosely, and she'll do all the work. I'll be right beside you."

"Gee whiz, this is great, isn't it, Jan? Boy, I wish I could ride a horse like you do." He looked up at Nick.

"If Doctor Rossi is taking care of you, you will. Five years ago I was sitting in that cart being pulled by a pony named Feather. If I can do it, so can you. Say *giddy-up* and Sally will take you wherever you want to go."

"Giddy-up, Sally," Benjie cried excitedly, his thin little hands shaking with the reins. Sally obediently trotted off.

"Hey, Nick," Derek shouted after them, "come back around noon and we'll have that picnic. I'm going to take Jan up into the hills to Prospector's Gap."

Nick signaled that he had heard and cantered beside the pony cart.

Derek grasped Jan's hand and led her around the house to the corral and barn. Two horses were already saddled and waiting.

As they rode side by side into the hills, Jan was once again aware of the beauty surrounding her. Derek pointed out a dry riverbed and said they were going to follow it into the hills, where she was certain to be surprised.

Long before they reached it, Jan could hear the joyous splash of water. The air became sweeter, more fragrant with greens, and lighter with moisture. As they rounded an outcropping of huge boulders, the sound of rushing water became louder. Eagerly, she dug her heels into her mount's flanks. When she saw it, she was overcome. Sunlight dazzled her and reflected off the waterfall in a crown of jewels. The pool into which the waterfall emptied played in the sunlight and winked back at the sun like a million Christmas tree lights.

Derek held back, watching the delight dance across Jan's features. There was no need for words; it was all there to be seen in her face. "You love the desert, don't you, Jan?"

"Oh, yes, I do. I never imagined that I would, but it's worked its magic on me."

"I wanted to bring you up here. It's one of my favorite places. Geologists say this used to be a rushing river that filled the whole valley. Now there's only this waterfall, which is fed by the un-

derground springs and empties into the pool. The
pool feeds that little brook, and I've heard it said
that the brook weaves its way across the desert and
all the way south to the Rio Grande.''

Jan was mesmerized, and it was with regret that
she followed Derek back down the hills to Bob
Rossi's house. Time had flown, and Nick and Benjie were returning for the picnic. Derek turned the
mounts over to Nick, who took them back to the
corral to water them. He lifted Benjie's crutches out
of the trunk space and help the boy down from the
pony cart, positioning the crutches under his arms.

"Think you can make it, buddy?"

"Yeah, sure, Derek," Benjie answered. "Just
lead me to the food! I'm starving!"

Around the back of the house was the swimming pool and a patio complete with picnic table
and benches. After lunch they rested in the shade of
the awning over the patio in companionable silence.

When Benjie began getting fidgety, Derek suggested Nick take him into the house and help him
get into bathing trunks so he could benefit from the
Jacuzzi.

While Nick and Benjie played a limited game of
water polo with a giant beach ball, Jan and Derek
prowled through the house. If possible, the house
was lovelier on the inside than outside. The ceilings were high, allowing the hot desert heat to rise,

leaving the cooler air below. Rafters and heavy beams were left exposed, and between them was plaster, roughened and swirled. The floors were red tiles and accented by frequent use of area rugs in wonderful patterns.

The house itself was larger than Jan had expected. Four bedrooms, den, living room, kitchen, dining room—each decorated uniquely and lovingly. "If I had a lot of money and didn't know what to do with it, I'd buy this place and live here forever and ever. I could paint and cook and just plain love it."

Derek smiled. "You really like it? You don't think it's too remote?"

"It wasn't too remote for Dr. Rossi, and he had to go into Phoenix every day. But I'm only dreaming—where would I ever get that kind of money? And even if it were possible, where would Ben go to school?"

"It's not as remote as you think," Derek explained. "This is even closer to Phoenix than the Rancho or the Golden Lasso. I have to confess, on the drive out this morning I took the long way around, using secondary roads. I thought you and Ben would enjoy an early morning ride. I could see you were nervous and tense when I picked you up; I thought the ride would relax you."

"That it did. I used the time to straighten a lot of things out in my head," Jan laughed merrily as Derek led her out onto the patio again.

"I'm glad, Jan." Derek looked off to the pool, where Nick and Benjie were having a rousing good time. "I'd better water and feed the pony, Sally. Nick has spent his whole day with Ben and probably hasn't done it yet. Want to give me a hand?"

Jan followed Derek around to the barn, where the cool shadows and fragrant straw beckoned them in from the bright sunshine.

Derek unhitched Sally and watered her. As she drank, he picked up a curry comb and smoothed the coat on Sally's flanks. Jan watched Derek's hands move over the animal in sure and gentle strokes. For a fleeting moment, she imagined the feel of Derek's hands on her own flesh and felt herself blush.

"I hope you have room for Sally and her little cart in your barn, Jan. I intend to make a gift of her to Ben."

Everything inside of Jan railed against Derek Bannon. This would be one more thing she would owe him. She could never have given Benjie a surprise like owning Sally—never in her whole life. And when she sold out the Rancho to Derek Bannon and eventually went back to New York, what then? He had made himself a part of Benjie's life, and she would have to cut him out. And he would have to leave Sally behind, too. She would be the bad guy in Benjie's eyes and he would never, ever forgive her.

Adrenaline shot through her and she became more angry than she had ever been in her entire life. She backed off a step and looked measuringly at Derek Bannon. "You are the cruelest man I've ever met, and I hate you for it!" she hissed. "I know what you're doing, and I'm the one who'll pay the price. I can never do the things you've done for Benjie. How could you do this? He's just a little boy and he loves you like a brother and he trusts you. When I take him back to New York, I'll be tearing his heart out. You're thoughtless and insidious and I hate you!"

"New York? You're taking Ben back to New York? Why? He's doing so well with his therapy..."

"Yes, back home," Jan snapped. "I've decided to sell you the Rancho at the end of your deadline. August first. And when I do, what do you think I'm going to do? Pitch a tent? Isn't this what you've intended from the very beginning? Well, you can have the ranch—for your original offer, not a penny more. I don't want anything from you, Derek Bannon. But," she said, pushing a finger into his chest, her eyes spewing fire, "you're the one who's going to tell Benjie, not me. I almost thought you were different there for a while, but you're not.

You're a user, Derek, and you prey on women and little children. So buzz off, Derek Bannon, and leave me and my brother alone," Jan cried, the tears running down her cheeks.

"Jan..." She paid him no heed, turning on her heel to head out of the barn. He caught at her arm and pulled backward. "Wait... you don't understand..."

"I understand, all right. I understand more than you think. Get away from me you...you...Arizona gigolo," she shouted, pulling herself free.

She nearly escaped him, thought she had, and the door to the barn was within reach, when she felt her ankles being swept out from under her and fell backward into a stack of hay in one of the stalls.

"Gigolo!" Derek shouted in rage, wrestling her onto her back and staring down into her face. "Of all the stupid, stubborn women..."

"That's it. Call me stupid. Well, I'm not stupid. I saw right through you from the beginning. You're stupid for what you're trying to do to my little brother! I'm one thing, but don't mess with Benjie. He loves you, and when I have to take him away he's going to be heartbroken."

Derek held her firmly, pressing her back into the fragrant straw, a wry smile playing about his mouth. "And does his sister love me?" he asked quietly.

"Love you!" she spit out. "I hate you! I wish I had never set eyes on you. You're disgusting. What kind of man are you anyway? I've seen the way you treat Andrea and here you are trying to...to..."

"Seduce you?" he asked, laughing, pressing his full weight on her to control her strugglings.

"Go away—leave me alone. But I'm warning you—I'm going to steal a page from your book and do as you suggested. You said I should let Benjie accept whatever life has in store for him. When he's devastated because of all this, I'll let him know exactly how you are. How dare you laugh at me?" Jan cried, gulping back the tears for a second time. "I'm warning you, get away from me," she said through clenched teeth as she was paralyzed into immobility as she watched Derek lean closer, holding her tighter, squeezing her between the haystack and himself.

"I mean it, get away from me. This is the last time I'm going to tell you...I'll scream." He lowered his head and covered her mouth with his.

There was no escaping him. He held her roughly, molding her body to his. Jan summoned all her determination to speak. "Leave me alone," she gasped as he lifted his mouth from hers. Her voice came out thin and weak—hardly the strong emotional statement that she had made to him a moment ago. But that was before he was looking at her as he was now. Before he had trapped her in his embrace and held her against him. So close, so very close.

Derek looked down at her and the world was in his eyes. Tenderly, he touched his finger to her chin, lifting her face to his. A tear slowly traced along her cheek, and he brushed it away. "You're trembling. Do I make you tremble, Jan?" His voice was soft and gentle, belying the strength in his arms. The sound of her name on his lips, the way he said it, sent a stirring through her veins. "Why do you think I'm such a dragon?" As if he hadn't expected her to answer, he pressed her head to his chest and held her, quieting her, soothing her, as though she were a wild colt.

Once again his finger tipped her face to his and he covered her mouth with his own, bringing her back in close contact with his lean, tall frame. Jan felt the hard, manly boldness of him, and she closed her eyes as his searing lips traced feathery patterns over her face and throat. His hands caressed her, leisurely arousing in her a varicolored array of emotions.

A warm, tingling tide of excitement and desire washed through her. Her mind whirled giddily and a soft sigh escaped her lips as she welcomed his kiss. Her trembling lips softened and parted as his mouth possessed hers. Her arms came around his back, aware of his strength and masculinity, and they held each other, offering to one another and blending together like forged steel. Their kisses became fierce and hungry, making them breathless.

Jan fought against the chaos in her mind. She should be fighting him, running away from him, raking her nails across his arrogant face. Instead, she lay back in his arms returning his kisses, bending her body against his, loving the touch of his mouth on hers, the touch of his hands on her neck, her throat, her breasts.

Clasping her tightly to him, as though he would draw her into himself, Jan felt the thunderous beating of his heart while her own pounded a new and rapid rhythm.

Their moment became an eternity before Derek loosened his hold on her. His eyes held her softly, with tenderness, and when he spoke, his voice was thick with emotion and husky with desire. "I'm not such a dragon, Jan. And I don't breathe fire on little boys or on their beautiful sisters."

Jan turned away, not able to bear the hurt she saw in Derek's eyes. She had hurt him cruelly when she had accused him of using Benjie.

Suddenly, as though a curtain had dropped between them, Derek regained his composure and usual cool tone. "I didn't mean for this to happen. I didn't want anything to spoil Ben's day."

Jan nodded in agreement, not able to face Derek. Benjie had been looking forward to this picnic, and the day was almost at an end. She didn't want to spoil it for him now any more than Derek did. He helped her to her feet and began to brush the hay from her back.

"I won't mention the pony to Ben. Perhaps you're right—I was being thoughtless." He took her arm and led her back to the patio, and Jan noticed a new, almost imperceptible possessiveness in the touch of his hand. And when he spoke to her the brittle tone of his anger was gone. While not exactly lighthearted, she heard herself reply in kind and she began to relax. Derek was as good as his word. Benjie's day wouldn't be spoiled by hidden currents of bitterness between them.

For the remainder of the day, Jan remembered the taste of his mouth on hers and the strange and wonderful emotions she had experienced in his arms. She basked in Derek's attention and reveled in the sound of Benjie's laughter. And at the end of the day, when they loaded into the car for the drive home, she was saddened that it had come to an end.

As Derek drove them home in the deepening twilight, Jan rested her head back against the seat and relived the moments she had shared in Derek's arms, and she knew with certainty that she would remember this day always.

Chapter Nine

Jan woke with a throbbing headache, knowing that the day was somehow going to bring disaster; she could feel it, sense it in every pore of her body. She felt drained as she swung her legs over the side of the bed. Drained and foolish. How could she have allowed Derek Bannon to do the thing he did—to kiss her like that, to touch her that way? She had behaved terribly, giving in to her emotions like some wanton hussy. "Oh, heaven," she cried, "how could I allow myself to..." It was over and done with. From this moment on she would make sure she was never within a mile of him. She would let an attorney handle the sale of Rancho Arroyo,

and she would never have to come in contact with
him again. At the end of the month she would be
back in New York and all of this would be behind
her. A brief interlude in her life—no more and no
less. She could do it; she had no other choice. If she
had to, she would work day and night, twenty-four
hours a day to make up to Benjie the loss he was
going to feel when Derek Bannon was no longer
around to serve as a big brother to him. Surely the
little boy would understand—or would he?

The cold, bracing shower helped a little in
brightening her spirits and so did the bright tan-
gerine pullover. However, Delilah's gloomy countenance in the kitchen dampened her fledgling
spirits. "Don't spare me—just tell me what's
wrong," Jan muttered as she sat down at the wide,
butcher-block table with a cup of coffee.

Delilah stood with her hands on her ample hips,
her dark eyes sad and gloomy. "Is bad. Freezer ruin
all food—Gus throw out now."

"What?" Jan exploded, knocking her coffee cup
onto the polished floor. "How could the freezer be
broken? And what happened to the emergency
generator? It can't be broken; the food can't be
spoiled—it just can't be. Tonight is the going-away
party for our guests. Are you sure, Delilah?"

"Yes, the fuses blew. No power all night. You
have to cancel party. Or you go to town and buy
more food. Guests expect big wing ding; you

promise on brochure. Everybody dress up and have good time. No good time," she said, shaking her black braids. "You have big problem."

The sound of Benjie's chair caught Jan's attention, and she immediately began to pour cereal into a bowl. Her hand trembled and she dropped the spoon as she set the dish in front of Benjie. He waited patiently for another moment and then gulped the sugary flakes as if he was in a hurry. "Why don't you call Derek and ask him if the guests can have dinner at the Golden Lasso? He told me he always keeps six tables in reserve for special guests. Do you want me to ask him?"

Jan stared at the little boy without seeing him. It was a solution. But where was she to get the money to pay for the night's entertainment? "No, don't ask him. I'll think about it. Is Dusty Baker taking you to the hospital or is Derek doing the driving?"

"I never know. Whoever shows up," Benjie said blithely as he put the chair in motion. "I'll see you this afternoon."

"Okay, Benjie. Have a good day." Jan sighed. It was the perfect solution, if Derek agreed. Maybe there would be some advance reservation checks in the mail, and she could make some kind of deal with him. And you weren't going to go within a mile of him, a niggling voice harassed. Sometimes we all have to do things we don't want to do, she answered herself.

By late morning the mail had arrived with a fifty-dollar check for a deposit for a family of three due to arrive in three weeks. She wouldn't be able to get inside the door of the Golden Lasso for fifty dollars. Could she lay her pride on the line and ask Derek Bannon for credit until the sale of the ranch went through? Oh, she could ask him, and he would look at her with those mocking eyes of his and be very gracious, not to mention condescending, and say, yes, of course, he would help her out. He'd probably take it one step further and pick up the tab himself, compliments of the Golden Lasso. She didn't need his charity and she didn't want it. But the guests—what was she to do?

Delilah was hovering, making Jan jittery to the point of exploding. "When you make phone call to Golden Lasso?" Delilah demanded. "Is late."

"Look, if I go to the guests and explain the situation, maybe they'll understand. I can offer them a refund at some future date," Jan said, grasping at straws.

"*Tsk, tsk, tsk.*" Delilah clucked her tongue. "You no understand. No food for any kind of dinner. They pay and want to eat. You want guests to go to bed hungry? *Tsk, tsk, tsk.*"

Jan was outraged. "Are you telling me there's no food at all? Nothing! What about the refrigerator?"

"Wienies," Delilah said curtly. "We have one string of wienies. The rest is what we serve for breakfast."

Jan stared at the cook and trudged dejectedly to the office. There were no options, no choices. She would have to call Derek Bannon and plead her case. Each time she reached for the phone she withdrew her hand, and then the sound of the children in the pool stiffened her spine, and she would again reach for the phone, only to draw away. Thank heaven the guests were leaving, and the new batch wasn't due to arrive till Sunday. Instead of sitting here like some ninny, she should be making calls, canceling the other reservations. She couldn't put it off any longer. She had just dialed the first three digits of the Golden Lasso when Delilah ran into the office. "You come see. Now. *Tsk, tsk, tsk,*" she said turning and waddling back to the kitchen.

"Oh, please let there be water." What *else* could it be. Everything that could possibly go wrong had gone wrong. When she walked into the kitchen, there was food everywhere, packed in ice. Good enough for an army. "Where, who... how..." she said to a broad-shouldered man hefting a heavy carton.

"You Jan Warren?" At Jan's nod he handed her a slip of paper. Tears burned her eyes as she scanned the brief, curt note. "Ben explained. Call this Arizona hospitality or, if you prefer, one businessman helping another.'' It was signed simply: DEREK BANNON. Darn! He must want something in return. Her ranch. No, she had already told him she was going to sell it to him. Protecting his investment ahead of time, that's what he was doing. And humiliating her in the bargain. She would have felt better if she had asked and arranged the terms. This made it sound like a gift—charity, for want of a better word. She didn't need his charity or want it. Yet she had to accept it. And she had to call him and acknowledge his generous help. That was going to be harder to do than asking for his help the way she had originally intended. When it came to Derek Bannon, she was always on the receiving end of things.

Jan thanked the delivery men and started to help Delilah stack the meats into the large kitchen refrigerator. Delilah was right—there was enough for an army. Evidently the illustrious Derek Bannon didn't want her weak from hunger when it came to signing on the dotted line. She hated herself for such opinions but didn't seem able to control her thoughts when it came to the owner of the Golden Lasso.

As soon as the cartons were emptied, Jan left the kitchen, needing no further reminders of Derek Bannon and wanting no more confrontations with her emotions. Perhaps a ride would clear away her

headache—if not clear it away, at least reduce it to
a dull ache. Delilah had things under control; Benjie wouldn't return for another three hours. She was
more or less on her own. Gus was seeing to the
freezer, and all the guests were doing their thing.
She shook her head as she saddled Soochie and admitted to herself that she didn't like the feeling of
not being needed. Everyone deserved to be needed.
Why should she be any different?

Tugging on the reins lightly, she let Soochie have
her head. The golden animal reared once and then
headed for the open. Jan sat the horse with ease,
reveling in the hot breeze the galloping animal created. She felt free, more free than she had felt since
coming to Arizona. She rode for what seemed like
hours before dismounting. She withdrew two ap-
ples from her saddle bags, gave one to the horse,
and started to munch on the other.

She felt so tired and yet she had done nothing
really physical since coming to this beautiful state.
Mentally tired, she corrected herself. How terrible
to be in love and not be able to do anything about
it. It was such a devastating feeling. How could you
love someone so much and not have the other person love you? Tears gathered and she wiped at them
with the back of her hand. That was another
thing—she had to stop this senseless weeping and
wailing every time she thought of Derek Bannon.
Crying never solved anything. All it did was give

you the hiccups and red-rimmed eyes. She fixed her watery gaze on the quiet horse and muttered, "Emotionally, I can't afford you, Derek Bannon."

The hot Arizona sun, along with the horse's quiet grazing made Jan drowsy. The past day's tensions evaporated as she fell into a deep, restful sleep. She neither saw nor heard Soochie as she trotted off on her own to explore the terrain.

Jan woke, stiff and disoriented, from her sound sleep to see darkness falling. What happened? she wondered wildly as she struggled to her feet. She rubbed grit from her eyes, and gradually her eyes became accustomed to the indigo shadows around her. It took her seconds to realize Soochie was gone. She whistled and called the mare to no avail. How far had she come? She had ridden for over two hours and an hour of that had been fast, hard riding. To go it on foot, providing she didn't get lost in the darkness, would take her more hours than she could stand. The blisters on her feet were not healed sufficiently to make the long trek back even if she were wearing rubber-soled canvas sneakers. What time was it? How long had she slept? Surely by now somebody should be looking for her. When she didn't show up for the guests' farewell party, someone would start wondering about her whereabouts. Benjie. Benjie would worry and call Derek. But they didn't know which way she had come. All they would know was that Soochie was gone.

She couldn't sit here all night and do nothing. She had to move. She had to try to find her way back on her own. How could she have been such a fool as to let the animal graze and not tether it? Why did she always have to learn her lessons the hard way? She wasn't going to find any answers sitting here.

She started out, her head high and her shoulders straight. She trudged for hours under the full moon, wishing a tall, blue-eyed man named Derek Bannon would swoop down on her and carry her back to the ranch. She sighed wearily. At this point she would settle for Gus and a painted wagon. She was tired! She had to keep going and not think. One foot in front of the other, over and over. The blisters on the backs of her heels were sore and running. Disgustedly, she removed the offending sneakers and hurled them into the darkness. The moment she did she was sorry. Alone and lost in the desert was bad enough. Barefoot, it was intolerable.

Twice within minutes she stumbled and fell. She managed to get to her feet and start walking, only to fall into a crumpled heap. Bitter tears of frustration rolled down her cheeks. She couldn't give in, not now. The highway must be close. A while ago she thought she had heard the engine of a car, but it was too dark to see anything with the moon sliding behind a giant cloud cover.

It was the feel of the macadam road on her sore, bare feet that told her she had finally found a road. Where it was, she had no idea. She shivered violently as she tumbled down the road. She prayed silently that she was going in the right direction.

Jan raised her eyes and for the first time was aware that dawn was fast approaching. She had been stumbling along with her head down and her eyes closed. Now she would be able to see where she was. Hopefully, a car would come along and offer her a ride.

Jan heard a car and teetered on her feet in an effort to steady herself. She was so tired and numb from the night air that she fell, skinning her hands and knees. Angry beyond belief, she pummeled the road with her clenched, bleeding hands. Why wasn't someone helping her? She had to get up and walk. The car—it was stopping. "Please, don't let it be a mugger," she gasped.

The voice was angry and... What was that in the tone that reminded her of her father? Who cared? She was picked up in strong arms and carried like a baby. That was okay—she felt like a baby with the tears running down her face. She knew she was safe; she could feel it even if the voice was chastising her.

"You aren't safe to let loose, do you know that?" the voice was saying over and over. "Half the state is out looking for you. How could you be so thoughtless, so careless, and for heaven's sake, don't you care about that little boy back at the ranch who is crying his eyes out over you?" And then the arms tightened around her.

She burrowed her head in his chest and muttered. "I care, I really do. I knew you'd find me. I want to go home—my feet hurt." And then she was asleep.

Derek gently lowered the sleeping Jan into the depths of the bucket seat. A smile played around his mouth as he watched her curl into a ball and then sigh. He fastened her seat belt securely and climbed behind the wheel. Before he fastened his own seat belt he bent over and touched Jan's tousled hair. He kissed her lightly on the mouth and heard her murmur in her sleep, "I knew you'd find me." He whistled softly as he slid in the clutch and headed back toward Rancho Arroyo.

Chapter Ten

Leaning back against a nest of pillows, Jan contemplated first the gray, overcast day through her window and then her bandaged feet, which were propped up with cushions at the foot of her bed. She had been guilty of some foolish moves in her life, but getting lost and trekking through the desert all night long was, without a doubt, the most stupid to date. What did Derek Bannon think of her now? She moaned. He had been so angry with her, so upset with her stupidity. And then her falling into his arms with such abandoned relief! Jan cringed and tried to make herself invisible by hiding under the bedcovers. She couldn't hide from

what she had done any more than she could forget
what a fool she was. It was over, done, and she was
safe once again in her own bed with a cup of black
rum tea at her elbow.

"Tsk, tsk, tsk..." Delilah muttered as she waddled into the room to check on her impatient patient. Deftly, she replaced Jan's bandaged feet on
the cushion and ordered her to remain in bed. "You
have a visitor in the lobby. I bring him to see you—
you don't get out of bed," she ordered as she exited into the hallway.

"No! Wait! I don't want... Oh... I don't want
to see Derek," Jan yelped. "Can't you see I'm a
mess? Just look at me! Delilah, please, don't bring
him up here. Look at this... this... thing I'm
wearing," Jan wailed, pointing to her oversized
football jersey with the number 77 printed across
the chest. "Delilahhhh!" she pleaded.

Delilah looked back and shrugged. "So, you
number seventy-seven on list. Is funny nightgown
but not my business," she shrugged again. "Your
visitor not Mr. Bannon but lady in tight pants. I
bring her tea and maybe cookies."

Jan's curiosity suddenly peaked. "What lady in
tight pants? Are you sure it isn't Derek and you're
only teasing me?"

"I sorry you disappointed, but I know lady when
I see one. You want to see Mr. Bannon, I call

Golden Lasso and tell him," Delilah clucked as she
closed the door behind her.

Jan settled back against the pillows, her pretty
features turned down into a frown. The visitor had
to be Andrea—who else could it be? Beautiful,
stunning Andrea. Jan slid beneath the covers and
pulled them to her chin. She'd die before she allowed Andrea to see the football jersey that doubled for a nightgown, especially since she had seen
the cloud of black lace that was part of Andrea's
wardrobe. Darn! Why did these things always happen to her?

A cautious knock on the door alerted Jan to Andrea's approach. "Come in," she called weakly.

"I came as soon as Derek told me what happened. I'm so sorry about what happened to you
last night. You must have been frightened to death.
Do you have any idea how lucky you are that Derek found you? You could still be out there wander-
ing. It was foolish, Jan, and it could have been a
fatal accident. I hope you're more careful in the
future."

Jan was puzzled. Andrea sounded so sincere, so
concerned. Would she still sound that way if she
knew that Jan, too, was in love with Derek? Not
likely. "I realize what a fool I was, and you don't
have to worry about me doing such a stupid thing
again. I really did learn my lesson." In spite of

herself, Jan found that she was warming to Andrea's sincere concern.

"We were all concerned about you. Especially your little brother. I can't tell you what the little guy went through when Derek had to tell him that they couldn't search for you during the night. You put Ben through a lot of anguish with your foolishness. Please." Andrea held up her hand to stifle Jan's protests. "I saw Ben and what he went through. He's told me about the accident that took your parents, and all he could think of was that something had happened to you, too! That was unfair, Jan, and Derek and I hope you'll take Ben's feelings into consideration in the future."

Jan bristled and she felt as though the hair at the nape of her neck was standing on end. How dare Andrea? How dare Derek? Who did they think they were? As if she had planned her bad luck the night before just to put Benjie through a bad time. If there was anyone in this world who could get Jan's back up, it was Derek Bannon and Andrea.

"This is hardly any of your business," Jan growled, her face stiffening into hard lines of anger.

"You're wrong, Jan. It is my business and Derek's too. We care about you and we love Ben." Exasperated, Andrea emitted a deep sigh. "Look, Jan, I didn't come here to stage an argument. I'd like us to be friends because we're neighbors, and we're so close in age a friendship would seem natural. But it's evident you aren't interested in my friendship, and I'm truly sorry for that. Derek's been pleading me to come over here and get to know you better. I tried to tell him you seemed less than receptive to the idea, and this will prove to him that I was right. However, just so my trip isn't wasted, I'd like to invite you and Ben to my wedding. It's the last Saturday in July. In the gardens at the Golden Lasso. I hope you'll put aside your hostility for me and bring Ben. I really want both of you to attend."

Jan couldn't believe what she was hearing. Derek had pleaded with Andrea to come over and try to be friends? After the times he had taken her in his arms, the way he had kissed her? He wanted her to be friends with his wife-to-be? Jan realized she was glaring at Andrea, who had turned her face away rather than subject herself to Jan's open hostility.

"Take care of yourself, Jan. Blisters can be a nasty problem. If there's anything I can do for you—"

Jan had turned her head away.

"I see. I don't know what I've done to make you feel this way about me, Jan. And I'm sorry." Not waiting for a reply, Andrea turned and left the room.

Jan sat and stewed until Delilah came back into her room. "Delilah. Do you know what she wanted?" Jan sputtered. "She had the gall to come here and rail me out for what happened last night. She told me what anguish I put Benjie through—as though I'd planned it! As though I wanted to scare the life out of him! And then, after telling me how stupid I was, she had the nerve to invite me to her wedding! Even after blaming me for the fact that she and I aren't friends!"

"Reason you're not friends is your fault," Delilah said calmly, puttering around the room with a tired old dust rag and flicking the cloth haphazardly over the surface of the furniture. "Sometime you have face like cigar store Indian. Much frown, much anger. Me, I think sometimes you scared, so I still like you. Other people, they don't understand like Delilah."

"Is that what you think?" Jan challenged.

"How else to think? That you really one nasty person? No, I think you scared sometimes," Delilah answered matter-of-factly, seeming to concentrate on flicking the dust cloth between the bottles of hand cream and perfume that dotted Jan's dresser. "You tell her that you go to wedding?"

"I did not! Why should I want to go to *her* wedding? I don't care that Derek told her to come here and make friends with me! And I don't care to go to the wedding!"

"Oh, sure. You only care that they very nice to Benjie. You only care that Mr. Bannon take Benjie to hospital for treatments. You only care that he come here at night to take care of boy because you can't. I see," Delilah said offhandedly, still busying herself with straightening the room.

Desperate to justify her decision without revealing the true reason to Delilah, Jan persisted. "What kind of people are they anyway? I have every reason to believe that Andrea is living in sin with—with—her fiancé. Just because they're going to get married now, is that reason enough for me to condone what they're doing? And to bring Benjie to that wedding?"

"Is reason enough because Mr. Bannon is good to you. You think somebody live in sin? Big deal!" Delilah snorted, stuffing the dust cloth into her apron pocket and coming to stand at the bedside. Her hands were propped on her hips and her shoe-button eyes snapped with anger. "You look at me, I live 'in sin' with Gus for forty years. Is nothing wrong with me. Is nothing wrong with Gus. We get married, we have plenty wrong. He tell me what to do and I have to do it. Now we live in sin. When I tell him, 'Buzz off, you old Indian,' he listens. I marry him and he stick like fly to honey. Is good for some, is not good for others. You not judge other people, Miss Warren. I go get you something to eat. Later I give you advice."

Delilah left Jan alone in the room, and the hard sound of the closing door announced the woman's anger. Jan pummeled her pillows. Maybe she really was "one nasty person," as Delilah had said. But how could she go to the wedding and watch the man she loved marry someone else? What kind of people were they? What kind of man was Derek Bannon? There he was about to marry Andrea, and yet he seemed bent on seducing Jan. And Andrea—openly flirting with Dusty Baker at the testimonial dinner! And on the plane! What kind of marriage was Andrea going to have? Maybe they were planning on having one of those open marriages. Well, she wasn't going to get involved. Never! A fresh wave of tears drowned out her hiccups as she continued to pound her pillows with a vengeance.

Nearly an hour later, exhausted from her crying, Jan dried her eyes and sat up in bed to gulp some coffee from the breakfast tray Delilah had set on her nightstand. The coffee was less than steaming, but it made little difference—she couldn't taste it anyway.

Within the past hour Jan had reached a decision. There was an old saying that when you were down and out the only way to go was up. Perhaps some people were cut out to be martyrs, but she wasn't one of them. People got married every day of the week; some of them lived happily ever after and some didn't. When she got married, if she ever did, she would live happily ever after because she wouldn't marry anyone who didn't love her as much as she loved him. How could that—that weasel kiss her until her teeth rattled and then go off and marry someone else? She sniffed and blew her nose with gusto.

The next step was to get out of bed—gingerly, of course—and hobble around and see to her business. Life didn't stop just because you were laid up in bed and were moaning about fate and the way the cards were being dealt. She would spend the rest of the day on the veranda at the back of the lodge with a tall glass of lemonade and the ledgers from her office. And she would try to force her thoughts to remember the finer details of the blue prints she had seen in Derek Bannon's apartment the night she had gotten him to help her with the sudden, terrifying cramps that had plagued Benjie. She had a right to know what Derek Bannon was planning for the Rancho Arroyo.

Climbing out of bed was less painful than she had imagined. Delilah's poultices were working their magic. She dressed in Levis and a colorful sleeveless blouse. Her feet were tender but not too painful, and she noticed the cane Delilah had brought for her so she wouldn't be putting her full weight on her blistered feet. Jan felt decrepit, old beyond her years, as she made her way down the stairs and through the lobby out to the veranda. Gratefully, she dropped into a wicker chair and winced with relief. She wasn't going to be doing much walking in the next few days, that was for sure.

By midafternoon Jan was certain of one thing. She was on the verge of bankruptcy. With the payment from the guests that were due within a few days, she would just be able to meet her expenses. That was providing nothing else went wrong.

Jan had just closed the last ledger when Delilah came to the door and motioned to the phone she was plugging into a jack on the veranda. "For you. They say they call from bank." Jan picked up the receiver, her heart leaping wildly.

"Janice Warren," she announced in her most businesslike tone.

"Miss Warren, this is Michael Davis at City Trust. The bank has approved your application for a loan using your house in New York as collateral. If you would care to stop by the bank sometime tomorrow, we can set the wheels in motion, and I can guarantee you'll have your money within ten days."

"Why, thank you, Mr. Davis," Jan said coolly, fighting to keep her excitement from creeping into her voice. "I'll come by tomorrow afternoon."

She was solvent again, or would be in ten days. Now she didn't have to sell out to Derek Bannon, who seemed all too greedy for her land. She wouldn't have to go back to New York and lick her wounds. She could stay in Arizona and so could Benjie. And the first thing she was going to do was hire reliable help to get this business off the ground in the proper manner. She would take a few business courses at night in the off season and learn whatever there was to learn about managing a resort. With just one phone call her world was right side up again. If Derek Bannon would call and say he decided not to marry Andrea, her life would be perfect. She stared at the black phone, willing it to ring, willing it to be Derek.

When the instrument shrilled, Jan's heart almost jumped from her chest. It couldn't...it couldn't...it must be! "Hello," she said cautiously, breathlessly.

"It's Neil, Jan."

"Neil! What a nice surprise," Jan stuttered, regaining her composure. What a fool she was to think that her prayers would be answered and that the voice she would hear would be Derek's. "How nice of you to call," she choked into the receiver. "How are you? How's the house? Nothing wrong, is there?" she asked anxiously. Just what she would need. She could imagine the old house in New York burning to the ground and then the bank refusing her the loan.

"I'm fine," Neil answered in brisk tones. "And your house was fine when I saw it this morning. I'm not in New York, Jan. I'm here in Arizona. I decided I couldn't live without you and here I am. Tell me how to get to the ranch, and I'll soon be walking through your door."

Jan was stunned. Neil in Phoenix? He couldn't possibly have chosen a worse time to pay her a visit. "How...how nice," she said, trying for a light tone. "It's very simple. Take the Interstate east and watch for the signs about thirty miles out. They point the way to Rancho Arroyo and the Golden Lasso."

"Gotcha," Neil assured her. "Tell me you missed me as much as I missed you. I'm going to sweep you right off your ever-lovin' feet. You got that?"

"Yes, I heard you. Neil, you should have told me you were coming so I could have prepared," Jan said tartly.

"And spoil the surprise? No way! I knew you'd be eager to see me right about now. I purposely planned it this way. From now on I'm not letting you out of my sight. And look, Jan, do us both a favor and keep the kid out of sight for a while. We have a lot of catching up to do. By the way, how is the kid?" Neil asked as an afterthought.

Jan's jaw tightened. "If you mean Benjie, he's fine. He's making remarkable progress with his therapy. I thought I told you that in my letters."

"Great, just great. Remember now, I want to spend my time with you, not the kid. By the way, I quit my job. I'm going to help you out there at the ranch. I've decided we're a team and teams work together. See you in a little while.''

Jan looked at the phone and winced. Team. He quit his job. He wanted to spend all his time with her. She shrugged. At least she'd have an escort to Andrea's wedding and wouldn't look like an unwanted old maid. Jan shook her head. What was wrong with her? Was she crazy? What did it matter whether or not she had an escort? To save face? What face? Derek Bannon certainly wouldn't be impressed; he'd be too busy with Andrea on their wedding day.

An hour later Jan watched from her chair on the veranda as Neil careened around the circular driveway on two wheels, finally bringing the rented Pinto automobile to a grinding halt. Jan shivered and frowned. What was wrong with Neil? Didn't he realize there may have been guests or children who could have been hurt by his reckless driving. Jan's frown deepened. She hadn't liked Neil's "surprise" visit, and the idea that he quit his job gave her cause for concern. What did he have on his mind? What was she going to do with him during his visit?

She watched with a kind of detached interest as Neil hopped from the car, resplendent in cowboy attire that some fast-talking salesman must have palmed off on him. No one dressed that way! Certainly no one here in Arizona. Perhaps on the backstage lot of a Hollywood studio Neil's outfit would have seemed natural, but certainly not here! Talk about Rhinestone Cowboys! Jan giggled as she likened Neil to a cross between Tom Mix and Gene Autry. If he said, "Howdy, pardner," she would laugh in his face.

Neil was up on the veranda, teetering on his high-heeled boots, before she could blink an eye, and he was sweeping her off her feet. "Howdy, pardner. What say we mosey out to the old corral and snatch a few quick kisses?"

"Neil, put me down! We don't have a corral, and we don't 'mosey' anywhere. We walk or we use the pickup. I'm not in the mood for kisses, quick or otherwise. You're behaving like Benjie. Now put me down!" she squealed.

"You haven't changed. I was just having a little fun," Neil said loudly. "I thought you'd be glad to see me."

"I am glad to see you, Neil. It's just that you're so exuberant. Sit down here—let's talk. What made you decide to come out here? Vacation?" she asked, mentally crossing her fingers. "What ever possessed you to quit your job? I thought you liked it! Who's looking after the house? You did make arrangements, didn't you?"

"Of course I did. My Aunt Mary is going to stop by there several times a week to check on things. As for my job, it was boring me to death, and all the challenge was gone. It was time to start looking around, so here I am. Why do I have the feeling you aren't happy to see me? I haven't seen you smile yet?"

Jan managed a wan smile for his benefit. "I guess I'm just a little tired. I've been working pretty hard lately, and I haven't had too much time to sit around and relax. We're taking a breather before another wave of guests descends on us. It's not easy running a dude ranch."

Neil rolled his eyes. "I saw the sign at the turn-off for that Golden Lasso. You never mentioned it in your letters. I'll bet it gives you a run for your money. It looks like a swinging place to me. Who owns it?"

"I do," said a voice from the screen door leading onto the veranda. Derek held the screen door open for Benjie and then stepped into the porch himself. Jan swallowed hard as she watched Benjie maneuver himself along on his crutches. The boy was looking in stark amazement at Neil, and it was apparent he wasn't pleased with Neil's turning up on the doorstep.

"Neil Connors," Neil said, introducing himself, holding out a too starkly white hand. Derek looked at the hand a moment and then covered it with his.

"Derek Bannon," Derek said curtly.

"Derek owns the Golden Lasso and the Bison football team," Benjie offered proudly, "and he introduced me to all the players. Dusty Baker is a good friend of mine, too."

"How are you, kid?" Neil asked, stepping over to and putting his arm around Benjie. The boy shrugged off his arm and moved out of Neil's reach. It was apparent Benjie wanted nothing to do with this interloper.

"Neil is a friend of mine from New York. He'll be staying with us for a while," Jan said softly, mostly for Benjie's benefit.

"We're engaged to be engaged, if you know what I mean," Neil said brashly, winking at Derek Bannon.

"Neil!" gasped Jan in exasperation. "We're not engaged!"

"Not right this minute, maybe, but we will be. Why do you think I came out here? You aren't getting away from me again. Nice meeting you, Banyon," Neil said jovially, as he took Jan's arm to lead her into the lobby.

"His name is Bannon, not Banyon," Benjie cried with a catch in his voice.

"See you tomorrow, Ben." Derek nodded in Jan's and Neil's direction and left the veranda, his back stiff and straight.

"Listen, little fella, it was rude of you to do that. Don't you ever correct your elders. And don't ever embarrass me like that again. You mind your manners and we'll get along just fine." Neil scolded through tight lips.

Benjie stared at Jan a moment and then headed for the kitchen and some of Delilah's cookies and buttermilk.

Jan's shoulders ached with tension. She should have defended Benjie right then and there, but somehow the words didn't come. The little boy had given her every opportunity to come to his defense and put Neil in his place and she had failed. Jan knew she had trouble and his name was Neil Connors.

"Who was that guy, anyway? What's he doing with your brother? Looks like one of those aces to me."

"He introduced himself to you. His name is Derek Bannon and he does own the Golden Lasso and the Bison team, just as Benjie told you," Jan retorted curtly. "I don't have to explain anything to you, Neil. Derek Bannon happens to be a very nice person. He's gone out of his way to take Benjie to the Phoenix Medical Center every day. Benjie is crazy about him."

"Yeah, and why are you so defensive of him?" Neil demanded, watching Jan very closely.

Jan hedged. "Am I? I told you, I think he's a very nice person, and he's been great with Benjie."

"Well, if he's been going out of his way to take the kid into the city for his treatments, I can relieve him of that chore right now. I'll take the kid from now on. That way you won't feel obligated to him."

"I don't feel obligated. He takes Benjie because he wants to take him. He offered—I didn't ask."

"I've seen guys like him before and believe me, they never do anything without a reason. Especially lugging some lame kid around. I'm a guy. I should know. You've always been such a babe in the woods, Jan. From now on just leave everything to me."

Jan turned in a fury and lashed out. "Don't you ever call Benjie a lame kid again. And I don't need you to tell me about men like Derek Bannon. Let it drop, Neil, before we say things to one another that we'll regret later. If you don't like Derek, keep your thoughts to yourself. Benjie likes him and so do I."

It was immediately apparent to Neil that he had overstepped the bounds in Jan's private life, a life that somehow involved Derek Bannon. "Okay, sorry if I offended you. If you and your brother like him, then I'm certain he's a great guy. End of matter, subject dropped." Neil grinned as he put his arm around her shoulder to draw her closer. "Look, how about a tour of the ranch?" Noticing her cane for the first time, he asked, "What's wrong?"

"My feet are a little tender. I've acquired some nasty blisters. It's not serious, just uncomfortable. I'll have Gus show you around and assign you a cabin."

"You mean I don't get to stay here in the lodge? That's where you stay, isn't it?" Neil leered.

"That's exactly what it means. Paying guests stay in the cabins. You *are* a paying guest, aren't you?" Jan challenged.

The leer vanished, replaced by a look of stunned surprise. He recovered quickly and grinned. "You didn't think I was going to freeload, did you?"

Again Jan hedged. "Can you ride, Neil?"

"I'm not an expert, but I've ridden the trails in New York the same as you. I think I can manage. Bring on your old Indian guide," he joked.

Jan turned and Gus was waiting patiently, just as he did everything. Benjie must have told the Indian about their new guest.

"Well, I'm ready if you are," Neil said, perching a ten-gallon hat on his head, covering his golden hair. He seemed uncomfortable with the hat, just as he seemed unfamiliar with the studded Western-cut shirt and narrow slacks that were stuffed into handsome Western boots that were too obviously new. Jan fought back a giggle at the ridiculous sight he made and even Gus turned his head. But not before Jan saw the wicked grin that ripped across the Indian's usually solemn visage.

Neil turned to follow Gus and then wheeled back toward Jan. "You didn't say how you like my Western togs. What do you think?"

"Neil, I can truthfully say those are the fanciest duds I've yet to see around here."

"Thought you'd like them. See you later."

Delilah stood framed in the doorway to the kitchen. *"Tsk, tsk, tsk.* Your friend smell like vanilla pudding," she chirped.

"What do you think of him, Delilah?"

"I tell you, that man very pretty. Maybe turn some girls' heads, but not mine. That man not make me itch, he give me rash!"

Jan's giggle turned into helpless laughter, doubling her over. "He's not so bad when you get to know him," she gasped between bouts of hilarity.

"That why you laugh at friend?" Delilah said tartly as she shook her head, a perplexed expression on her face.

"Okay, okay, I shouldn't laugh, but he actually thinks that's the way cowboys dress. With bangles and beads. I can't help it. I think it's so funny!"

Delilah held her hands over her ample belly and joined in Jan's laughter. "I see but I not believe. First time I see Gus laugh in many years."

* * *

Jan dressed for dinner in a raspberry silk shirt
and tan slacks. She added a belt of natural twine
braid and stepped back to admire the effect. She
wasn't going anywhere but to the dining room in
the lodge so it didn't really matter how she looked.
Neil never noticed other people's clothes, and right
now he was overly impressed with his own flam-
boyant "togs," as he called them. Neil probably
thought of himself as a dandy, but once the ranch
hands got a look at him, they'd know him for what
he was. A dude. A genuine, bona fide eastern dude.

How had Derek looked when he saw Neil on the
veranda with her? Angry, amused, startled? He
looked, she decided, as though he was barely con-
trolling his anger. Serves him right, she mused. Did
Derek really think no other man in the world could
find her attractive? And when Neil had made that
brash statement about them being engaged to be
engaged, what was the expression that crossed his
face then? Jealousy? Jan sighed. The probability of
Derek being jealous of Neil was so farfetched as to
be ridiculous. At this point in time it made little
difference. Derek was getting married at the end of
the month, and Neil was going to save the day by
escorting her to that wedding. Afterward, she
would tell Neil there was no hope of furthering their
relationship as he had implied. If there was one
thing she knew, it was that she would rather end up

an old maid than settle down with Neil Connors. It would be like driving a wedge between herself and Benjie. There was little to say about the relationship between Neil and her brother. There was no relationship. Period.

If it was a spinster she was meant to be, then a spinster it would be. A vision of herself rocking sedately at the age of eighty-five with nothing to carry her through the days but the old memories of Derek Bannon kissing her and the feelings he evoked in her was such a vivid picture she winced. She clenched her small hands into tight fists and brought them crashing down onto her dressing table. The pain was welcome. If she wasn't careful, she could end up a basket case with Delilah spoonfeeding her.

With the aid of her cane Jan made her way onto the veranda to wait for Neil. Benjie was already there, watching a small portable TV that Gus had rigged for him. The small boy turned to his sister and with a break in his voice asked, "How long is he staying?"

Jan ruffled Benjie's hair and smiled. "Not long. I want you to be polite. I can't force you to like Neil, but I want you to be courteous. He is our guest. What are you watching?"

"It's an environmental program that Derek told me to watch. He said he thought I might find it interesting. He's really smart, Jan. He knows what I like and what I don't like. I don't even have to tell him. He's a super guy. He never gets mad and he always explains things to me. He explains even when I don't ask him questions. He listens to me and he hears what I say."

"You really do like him, don't you?" Jan said softly.

"You bet I do. Derek is my friend. He said he'll always be my friend, no matter what happens. And I can always count on him. That makes him a good friend, doesn't it?"

"I'd say so," Jan replied quietly. No matter what happens—now what did Derek mean by that? Probably his marriage to Andrea.

"You don't like him as much as I do, I can tell," Benjie complained.

"I like him, Benjie. It's just that with me it's different than it is with you. You're a little boy, Derek is a man. He relates to you differently that he does to me. I'm a girl." She smiled.

"Derek says some women are wily and tricky, and they like to manipulate men. That means to wrap them around their fingers. I had to get Derek to explain that to me because I didn't understand. He said that some women—like you, Jan—aren't like that at all. He said it's something dumb women have to practice."

Jan flushed. So Derek thought she was dumb and she hadn't practiced enough. Of all the insufferable, egotistical men, he took the prize. "Is that what he said?" Jan muttered through clenched teeth.

"Yeah. But Derek likes ladies. He said they make the world go round."

Jan gulped. She had to put an end to this conversation and now, before Neil made his appearance. "What do you feel like having for dinner?" she asked lightly.

"A hamburger, french fries, and a Coke," Benjie said, rattling off his favorite menu, knowing full well he wasn't going to get it. "But, I'll settle for roast beef and baked potatoes. Delilah said that's what she was making. And strawberry rhubarb pie. She made an extra one for Derek. I'm going to give it to him tomorrow when he picks me up. It's his favorite."

"What's who's favorite, sport?" Neil inquired as he walked up to Benjie clad in another brand new set of togs.

"Derek likes strawberry rhubarb pie, and Delilah made an extra one for me to give him tomorrow," Benjie said curtly.

"Listen, sport, you won't have to do that. Now that I'm here I'm going to take you to the hospital for your treatments. It's the least I can do for your sister to show her my appreciation. Your friend Derek can have some time off. Sometimes squiring little kids around can be a real drag. Running that fancy hotel up the road must take a lot of time. I'm sure he'd appreciate the time off. It's settled then," Neil said, looking from Jan to Benjie. Both remained mute, stunned at his words. He did have a point, Jan thought. It was impossible to read Benjie's face as he stared at the small screen.

As far as Jan was concerned, dinner was a dismal affair. Benjie picked at his food and stirred it around his plate with the fork, making scraping noises on the plate. Jan ate little, watching Neil wolf down his food and go back for seconds. Somehow he managed to keep up a running conversation dealing with things he saw wrong and how they could be improved.

"The way I see it, you have a thriving little investment here, and with the proper management you could do a lot better, Jan. You could add at least another dozen cabins and make them closer together. Of course, you'll have to cut back on some of the nature trails and cut down some of the timber, but in the end your bank balance will win out."

"Environmentally, it's not a good idea," Benjie said hotly. "We have to keep the trees and the trails. If Uncle Jake wanted to build on, he would have. Even Derek said people are ruining this country just so rich men can get richer."

Neil's voice rose an octave. "And who is it that owns that glittering neon palace down the road? He must have cut down a good many trees to build that! What's good for him is only good for him and no one else."

"That's a lie!" Benjie said belligerently. Before Jan could gather her wits about her, Benjie had his wheelchair backed away from the table and was whizzing through the dining area and out the wide doors to the patio and pool area.

"Opinionated little bugger, isn't he?" Neil managed through bits of Delilah's pie.

"Why shouldn't he be? Derek Bannon is his friend and that means a lot to Benjie. You attacked Derek and he didn't like it, so he defended the man the only way he knew how. You're too blunt, Neil. And for the rest of your stay here I don't want you to antagonize him anymore. He has enough to contend with as it it."

"Okay, okay. If you want to coddle him that's your business. If you remember correctly that was our problem back in New York. You worry about the kid too much. I'm here now, and I want you to worry about me and show me some consideration. Listen, I have a great idea. Let's go to Bannon's place and make up for lost time. A few drinks and take in the floor show. If you're such a good friend of his, maybe the guy will pick up the tab and it won't cost us a cent. What do you say?"

"Not tonight, Neil. If you want, you can go. I wouldn't be able to dance with the blisters on my feet, and you know I'm a one-drink person."

"Would you mind if I go?" Neil asked hopefully.

"Of course I don't mind. I have a book I want to read, and Benjie and I try to spend some time in the evening together since he's at the hospital most of the day. You go ahead and have a good time. I'll see you in the morning."

"You're terrific. That's why I came here." He swallowed the last of his coffee and rose from the table. Bending over Jan, he gave her a slapdash kiss and was gone before she could speculate on his hasty behavior.

Delilah stood over the table with her hands on her hips, making it clear that she had something to say. It was also clear to Jan that the woman wasn't going to speak until invited. Whatever it was, it must be a shocker, Jan thought. "So say it already," she said wearily.

"Your friend is phony and a freeloader. Gus no like, Benjie no like, and I no like," she said forcefully. "He stay too long, I quit."

"He's just visiting for a while," Jan said hotly, hating herself for defending Neil. She didn't like him either; he didn't belong here, and if it came right down to the matter, she would rather go to the wedding alone than go with him. How had this

happened? Why hadn't Neil called her first before
making the trip? She couldn't dwell on the matter
now. "We're just going to have to wing it for a
while. You can't quit and you know it. Gus
wouldn't let you. I'll keep Neil in line and see that
he doesn't bother you. What makes you think he's
a freeloader?" she asked curiously. "He's going to
pay like any other guest."

"No see deposit in book for money. I check out
his room," Delilah said slyly. "Much credit cards.
No bank book. No cash money. Everything new,
still tickets hooked on clothes."

"Shame on you, Delilah. You were spying on
Neil. Don't do it anymore," she said sternly, trying hard not to smile at Delilah's indignation.

Delilah sniffed. "You see—he go to Golden
Lasso and pick up . . . how you say . . . chick."

This time Jan did laugh and so did Delilah. "If
he does it might be the best thing that happens
around here. And I didn't have a chance to get a
deposit from him. He just got here. We do take
American Express, you know."

"For you, big problem," Delilah muttered as she
started to clear away the dinner table. "Your friend
a gigolo."

The frown on Benjie's sleeping face tore at Jan's
heart. He didn't like Neil and he saw him as a threat
to his and Jan's security. Somehow, tomorrow, she

was going to have to try to make him understand that Neil was just visiting and nothing was going to come of his visit in the way of a romantic entanglement for herself.

Jan adjusted the thermostat on the air conditioner and straightened the covers. Benjie stirred slightly, muttering something indistinguishable in his sleep. She waited to see if he would wake, and when he didn't, she released a sigh of relief. Turning off the lamp, she closed the door softly behind her.

A quick glance at her watch told her Neil would be just about ready to leave for the Golden Lasso. If she stayed in her room, she could avoid a meeting with him and at the same time she could make the call to Derek she was dreading. There was no reason to put it off, no reason for her to dread telling the club owner that the bank had agreed to her loan application. As one business person to another, he should be happy that she wasn't going to go under and had another chance at making the Rancho Arroyo a paying proposition.

Was it the phone call she was dreading or was it the sound of Derek's voice that was making her stomach churn and her heart pound like a triphammer? Twice she picked up the receiver and twice she replace it. Her throat felt dry, so dry she could barely swallow. Maybe, if she cleared her throat and took a sip of water from the bathroom it would help. Nothing would help. Do it and get it over with and go on from there. How would he take the news, she wondered fretfully. Just how badly did he want Rancho Arroyo and for what? A vision of the blueprints on Derek's desk floated before her. The worst he could think was that she was wishy-washy and unable to make up her mind. So what if her credibility came under his close scrutiny. She shouldn't care, but she did, even knowing he was marrying Andrea. She cared; it was as simple as that.

Dial the number, a niggling voice urged. Dial it and say what you have to say and hang up. Do it! Jan dialed the number Derek had given her and waited. Six, seven rings—he must not be home. Eight. "Hello."

"Derek, this is Jan Warren. I hope I didn't take you away from anything. I was just about to hang up."

"Is something wrong? Is Ben all right?" Derek asked in concern.

"Benjie is fine; that's not why I called. I called to tell you that I won't be selling the ranch after all. I applied to the bank for a loan, and they called today to say my application was approved. I'm sure that you understand and you won't hold it against me if I have to go back on my word to you. I have to do what's best for Benjie, and staying here and trying to make a go of the ranch is what I have to do. Your offer was more than generous, but I want you to know that I would have sold it to you for the original offer. I wasn't trying to hold you up or gouge a higher price out of you. Your original offer was more than fair." Jan's hand was clutched so tight on the receiver her knuckles were white as she waited intently for his reply. The creak of the floorboard outside her room didn't register. Neil's shadow in the dim light also went unnoticed as Jan waited.

"I understand, Jan. In a way it was my own fault. I apologize for placing a deadline on the transaction. If you decide to sell at some later time, I hope you'll give me first consideration. And I do hope that you can successfully make a go of the ranch for your own sake as well as your brother's. Good luck."

Jan blinked and looked at the receiver, a foolish look on her face. He certainly had accepted the matter better than she could have hoped for. He was even gracious and he had apologized. And she had worked herself into a frenzy over the matter. Men! He was probably in some kind of tizzy with his fast-approaching wedding and had other things on his mind. Which, she thought tartly, just went to prove that he probably didn't want the ranch so much after all. It would have been just another investment to him. What did he care about her or the people who worked here? Investments, tax dollars,

write-offs—that was all people like Derek Bannon
thought of. Lust—she had to add lust to the list.
And as long as she was making a list, she could add
cheating on Andrea and heaven only knew what
else. A philanderer, that's what he was. Well, she
wasn't going to cry over Derek Bannon. Her days
of crying were over. She was going to go on about
her life without him.

Darn! She forgot to tell him not to pick Benjie up
in the morning. She picked up the phone and then
replaced it. She couldn't, she wouldn't, make the
second call. She couldn't bear to hear his voice a
second time in one night, and this time she would
be the one who had to apologize. She would explain in the morning when he arrived for Benjie. It
would be harder to do face to face, but she would
do it. She wasn't a coward. Derek would be annoyed and justifiably so, but he would have to live
with his annoyance. She had been forced to live
with things over the past weeks that she didn't like
and he could do the same.

While she prepared for bed and brushed her
teeth, she wondered how long Neil was going to
stay. She made a mental note to ask him point-
blank on the morrow. She hoped she wouldn't be
forced to ask him for an advance payment. Surely
he would offer it on his own. He couldn't think he
was a nonpaying guest. She would explain, and if
he didn't like it, he, too, would have to live with his

annoyance at her blunt business manner. She was in business to make money, not give it away. Neil was going to be a problem in more ways than one—she could sense it, feel it in every pore of her body. She would be diplomatic, of course, but she wouldn't beat around the bush with him. How had she ever seriously considered him a possible suitor? She shook her head wearily and slipped into her football jersey.

If she had anything to be thankful for this day, it was that she hadn't paid much attention to her feet. What with the news from the bank and Neil's appearance and Benjie's apprehensions, her feet had stopped hurting. Delilah's herbal bandages had worked their magic, she thought to herself as she slipped beneath the covers.

Jan tossed and turned in her sleep. On the brink of wakefulness, she thought she heard a sound outside her window. Groggily, she crawled from the bed and slipped open her window. She wiped her eyes, trying to clear them and to see into the inky darkness outside. Leaning over the sill, she was stunned at the sight that greeted her. Neil and a girl—obviously a showgirl from the Golden Lasso from the looks of her costume—were chasing around the perimeters of the swimming pool. From where Jan stood, she could make out the bare flash of long, silky leg as the girl scampered away from Neil. Eventually, she allowed Neil to catch her, and

Jan flushed at the ardent kiss he was bestowing on the willing girl. His arms around her, he led her toward the trail that led to his cabin. His first night in Arizona and he had made a conquest. Suddenly, Jan hated him. She hated all men.

Slamming the window shut, she paced around the room. What she should do was march right over to Neil's cabin and tell him that she didn't run that kind of place and that if he wanted that kind of extracurricular activity he would have to go somewhere else. This was a family place! That was what she should do, but she wouldn't. But she was going to let him know what she had seen. She wouldn't put up with it—especially not around Benjie. If necessary, she would move Neil into the bunkhouse with the other hands for the remainder of his stay. Gus would keep him on the straight and narrow.

Jan tumbled back into bed. Move him out! By rights, she should throw him out! Out! Right off the Rancho! It didn't seem as though Neil was going to pay for his stay at the Rancho anyway. What did she have to lose?

Escorting her to the wedding so she wouldn't look like an undesirable old maid was no reason... "Oh, *no!*" Jan cried aloud. Here she was thinking she could hide herself from Derek and Andrea behind a seemingly interested suitor, and all the while that suitor was up at the Golden Lasso flirting with the showgirls. She would look more than ever like a fool! Jan's face became heated and red and she felt as though it could light up the dark corners of her lonely room.

Chapter Eleven

The following morning brought a fresh set of problems in the way of Delilah and Gus. When Jan entered the dining room for breakfast, Benjie was already seated at the table, his tight little face an indication of what the day was going to be like.

"Where's breakfast, Benjie? It doesn't smell as though anything is cooking," Jan said, a note of apprehension in her voice.

"That's because there isn't any breakfast cooking. We're having cold cereal and Gus is fixing it."

"Is Delilah sick? What's wrong?" Jan demanded, heading for the kitchen.

"I quit is what's the matter," Delilah announced as she pulled a heavy suitcase through the doorway.

"Why? What's wrong? What's happened this time?"

Delilah sniffed disdainfully and pranced for the lobby.

"Delilah, I demand an answer!"

The rotund woman turned and her dark eyes snapped at Jan. "You say living in sin is not good for young boy. You say it is wrong. Right? So I tell that old Indian that I want to marry, don't want to live in sin anymore."

Jan turned to Gus, who was pouring milk over Benjie's cereal. "And what did you say, Gus?" she asked, feeling more like a monkey in the middle by the moment.

"Darn fool woman," Gus growled. "She said she wanted to get married so I said okay. Now she's changed her mind. I won't ask her again."

"Not what he said at all," Delilah said angrily. "he say we have big Indian wedding. Humph! Me not stupid Indian woman. I know the law. Indian wedding not count for that!" she snapped her fingers. "Indian wedding is nothing. Must have license...everything! So I tell the old man Delilah only get married in Presbyterian church or nothing."

"You're throwing away a chance for Gus to marry you because of that?" Jan said incredulously. "I thought you said you didn't want to get married. Something about a fly sticking to honey. Which is it?" she asked wearily.

"So, I change my mind. Church wedding, marriage license, or nothing. Gus has one foot in happy hunting grounds. When he go, I want Social Security."

"I don't believe this," Jan said, rubbing her temples wearily. "Why can't you two get married because you love each other? Why do you have to put each other through all this torment?"

"I tell you if we marry we have problems," Delilah groaned.

"What's wrong with the Presbyterian Church, Gus?" Jan asked.

"Indian wedding or nothing," the Indian answered flatly.

"No, you wrong. Presbyterian church or nothing," Delilah shot back hotly.

"Then it's nothing," Gus muttered, stalking from the room.

"Why don't you have them compromise and get married by the justice of the peace and have an Indian reception afterward?" Derek asked as he walked into the dining room. Jan groaned in echo to Delilah's groan. Why did he always show up when she was in a spot? This time she was grateful for his advice. She didn't need a rebellious cook and a surly handyman.

"What do you say, Delilah? A justice of the peace sounds good to me. You give a little, Gus gives a little."

"No problem with Social Security later on?" Delilah demanded of Derek.

Derek grinned. "No problem. I guarantee it."

"Then it's settled," Jan said gratefully. "All you have to do is decide on a date and that's it."

"Is good thinking," Delilah said, waddling back to the kitchen pushing her heavy suitcase in front of her.

"Is Ben ready?" Derek asked. "I've got the car running."

"I could eat a horse! Where's breakfast?" Neil interrupted as he entered the room, rubbing his hands together briskly as though he were expecting to sit down to a long-awaited meal. "Oh, Bannon, are you here to take Benjie? No need, old buddy. I'll be doing it from now on. Jan wanted to stop by the hospital and see one of her employees, and I offered to drive. Right, Jan? Get you off the hook, Bannon," he said loudly, slapping Derek soundly on the back.

Derek's eyes narrowed as he stared first at Neil and then at Jan.

Jan felt her heart race up to her throat, and she felt powerless to tear her gaze away from Derek's.

She had to say something. Derek didn't wait. He turned on his heel and stalked out the door.

Feeling as though she'd been kicked in the stomach, Jan watched him leave. She had never seen Derek look at her like that, as though he hated her. And Benjie was avoiding her glance, his own mouth grim and tight. She might have one problem solved, but she had another now, a worse one.

"When do we eat? Who's cooking?"

"Whenever you want to eat, as long as you cook it, Neil. Delilah is taking the morning off. And from now on, Neil, you either get here on time for breakfast or you'll cook it yourself. Even when we're full with guests, breakfast is served between certain times. Anything else would be less than fair to Delilah. By the way, Neil, I'd like to have your American Express card so I can properly bill you for your stay here. Give it to me now so I can take care of the paperwork while you prepare your breakfast."

"My American Express card!" Neil said in surprise. "Do you mean you're really going to charge me for my stay here? And I still have to make my own breakfast? I came here, Jan, to see you, and I intend to help out in order to earn my keep." He laughed as he made his statements.

"I'm sorry, Neil. I don't operate a give-away establishment, and after today you'll have to move into the bunkhouse with the other hands. If it was a job you wanted, you could have said so from the beginning. Also, all hands eat in the kitchen; ask the men what time. You'll be sitting at their table from now on."

"Move me to the bunkhouse? But I like that cabin—it affords me privacy, and I won't be in your hair," Neil said, a note of panic in his voice.

"I'll just bet you like your privacy," Jan said tartly, remembering the scene below her bedroom window in the wee hours of the morning. "I'm sorry, but hands stay in the bunkhouse. Also, there are guests arriving in the morning. The cabins have been reserved. I can't let them down now. In case you don't understand, I'm in business to make money, not to give it away. That cabin has to be free to accommodate a guest."

"Is it reserved?" Neil demanded.

"No, not yet. But if I have an opportunity to take a reservation for it, I will."

"If that's the way you feel about it, here," Neil said, whipping out the plastic credit card. Jan accepted it and walked to the office, praying that the card was good. Neil was angry and behaving like a spoiled child. Her original instincts about him had been correct. He had thought he was going to be her guest in every sense of the word. What would he do and say when he realized that she had seen him bring the showgirl to his cabin? Somehow she knew he would try to weasel out of that, too.

* * *

Neil stayed in attendance while Benjie had his physical therapy as soon as he realized that was what Derek Bannon had always done. Benjie had protested, saying that it wasn't necessary, that he could make out just fine on his own. But Neil had insisted.

Jan took the opportunity to visit Andy Stone.

"Don't say it." The cowboy grinned as he watched Jan eye the apparatus that held his leg in its sling. "You aren't going to believe this, but I'm having the time of my life. There's this great little nurse on the three-to-eleven shift and she adores me. All she wants to do is give me sponge baths and back rubs. She says I'm her most willing patient."

"Just what I need, another wedding. Well, they say it always goes in threes," Jan grimaced.

"Who's getting married?"

"Delilah and Derek Bannon."

Andy laughed raucously. "Somehow I didn't think Delilah was his type!"

Jan laughed in spite of herself. "No, silly, not Delilah and Derek. Delilah and Gus and, of course, Derek Bannon."

Andy Stone whistled softly. "Derek Bannon is getting married? I didn't think there was a woman good enough for him. Surprises me that he's finally going to tie the knot. He's the sort of guy you always expect to end up a bachelor."

"Same difference. Marriage won't change anything for him."

"Aha, so that's the way the wind blows. You fell for the guy, right? Look, Jan, this is none of my business but you're real people. Down home. Bannon is in a different league. I'm real sorry you got hurt."

"Andy, I've known what you think of Derek right from the first time I met you at the airport. But, believe it or not, he does have his saving graces. Did you know he's been bringing Benjie in for his therapy almost every day. Not only that, but he saw Benjie through some pretty bad times. I walked into that whole thing with my eyes wide open. I've been hurt before and lived through it. What do you think about Delilah and Gus?" she asked, hoping to change the subject.

"I never thought she'd get married either. What did she do? Club Gus over the head? He's pretty set in his ways, Jan. Do you think he can handle a piece of paper that says he belongs to Delilah?"

"It was touch and go there for a while, but I think he's going to come around. Gus wanted an Indian wedding and Delilah was holding out for a Presbyterian church. I think they're going with the justice of the peace and then an Indian reception."

"When is the wedding? I hope I'm out of here. I want to give the bride away." Andy grinned. "Delilah's been good to me. Almost like a mother.

You should have been there the day I tried to explain the Social Security system to her.''

''Let me be the first to tell you that you got through to her loud and clear.'' Laughing and giggling, Jan explained about the meeting in the kitchen that morning. She felt happy sitting here with Andy, and it was with regret when an hour later she had to leave when the nurse said that visiting hours were over.

The ride back to the ranch was made in silence except for Neil's comments from time to time. Jan hated the sour look on Benjie's face and wondered if her own countenance was similar. This was best, she kept telling herself. Benjie had to be weaned from Derek's company sooner or later because when he got married he would forget the little boy. And, she thought bitterly, let's not forget the honeymoon. Benjie had said just a few days ago that Andrea said the honeymoon was thirty days in Europe. Wearily she closed her eyes. This was the best solution, the only solution, for both of them.

Her plan to hire summer college students to help at the ranch could now be put into effect. One of the stipulations for the job would be that Benjie be kept occupied. Hopefully, Benjie would be able to relate to the young people. If not, then she would have to come up with some other plan, but she would cross that bridge when she came to it. She was going to do the best she could by her brother and what more could anyone ask or expect of her?

"We're home Benjie. I'll get Gus to help you into the Jacuzzi for your thirty minutes."

"Help me out of the car, I'm tired." Benjie complained.

Jan frowned. He did look tired—as a matter of fact, he looked utterly exhausted. "Okay, I'll help you today, but after this you have to do it yourself. Is that understood?" Benjie ignored her as she and Neil struggled with his limp form. He made no effort at all to maneuver himself into his wheelchair.

The minuite he was out of sight Neil reached for Jan's arm. "I thought you said he was doing well and would be walking soon. He looks the same to me and that therapy session was a waste of three hours. Are you sure you aren't pouring your money down the drain?"

"The doctor says he's coming along nicely, and I'm not concerned about spending the money for Benjie's treatments, so don't worry about it. Benjie's just tired—those therapy sessions are hard on him—and he still has the Jacuzzi to get through. He's doing remarkably well, and I have every confidence in the doctor's prognosis."

"Exactly what is the doctor's prognosis?" Neil asked intently.

"That with proper treatment over an extended period of time Benjie will walk again," Jan said curtly. "Why?"

"I'm concerned over the little tyke. After all, we may one day soon decide to take that fateful step, and I want what's best for the kid just as much as you do. I'm not callous, you know."

"What fateful step are you talking about?" Jan asked, remembering the girl from the Lasso in the pool area.

Neil appeared flustered. "You know—we're engaged to be engaged—that sort of thing. I'm certainly willing to marry you if you decide that it's what you want. I wanted to give you enough time to get Benjie squared away before I asked you for a commitment. We'll work something out. Later," he added hastily.

Jan pretended puzzlement. "Work something out. Oh, I see, you mean you'll try to fit me in between visits to the Golden Lasso and all those luscious beauties scampering around. Thanks, but no thanks. I really think it's my destiny to be an old maid. A rich old maid," she added viciously as she stormed into the lobby. Of all the gall. Did she wear some invisible sign that she was good enough for certain men when they didn't have anything better to do. Bitter tears of frustration burned her eyes at the thought.

Nonchalantly, she looked around. Neil hadn't even bothered to follow her inside to say something trite, as was his manner when she got the upper hand.

She felt angry and humiliated as she plopped down on the swivel chair behind the desk.

Delilah marched into the room, a broom in one hand and the mail in the other. She laid the mail on the desk and turned to leave.

"Delilah, I've been thinking. I don't think you should get married after all. Men are terrible and they take advantage of women. We don't do that to them. I want you to think about it some more before you decide for sure."

Delilah's eyes widened. "First, you say live in sin no good; then you say marry and live happy life. Now you say sin okay. I want Social Security and real wedding. Gus agree to all my demands. If I chicken out now, I make fool of myself."

"Don't you see? That's the whole point. All we women ever seem to do is make fools of ourselves over men. Do you really want to get married or not? If you don't want to get married, then don't do it."

"How else I get Social Security?"

"Didn't Andy explain to you that my uncle, and now I, pay your Social Security? You can collect on your own without marrying Gus. Look," Jan said patiently, "all I'm trying to tell you is don't get married for the wrong reasons. If you love Gus and want to get married, that's fine. If you're marrying him for his Social Security, that's the wrong reason."

"Gus have many...how you say...defects," Delilah said, comimg up with the right word. "He sometime drink too much and no good for much."

"That's another thing. If he's drunk all the time, how do you handle it?" Jan asked.

Delilah shrugged and grinned toothily. "For me no problem. I put him to bed and play with him later."

In spite of herself Jan laughed. "Do what you want, Delilah, but make sure it's what you really want. And don't worry about your Social Security—it's all taken care of. Where are you going with that broom?"

"I chase Gus to help Benjie."

"Why didn't you just tell him instead of going after him with the broom?" Jan asked, knowing she wasn't going to like the answer.

"And have Gus think I not love him? Shame," she said, wagging her finger under Jan's nose. "Gus expect me to go after him. He like it when I chase him. Is love game we play. Like when you get lost in desert and Mr. Bannon come for you. Was big trick you play, no?"

"No, it wasn't a trick. I really was lost."

"I hear that story before. All young guests that come to ranch do that so Andy go after them." Delilah sniffed as she marched from the room, the broom held straight in front of her.

Chapter Twelve

The days continued to pass, each of them bringing Jan closer to having to attend Andrea's wedding. There were, however, several distractions that proved to be welcome. Another wave of guests arrived at Rancho Arroyo. With the help of two part-time workers things were working out nicely. Andy would be home from the hospital in another week, complete with a walking cast. Although he would be unable to resume his strenuous activities, his advice and know-how would be invaluable.

Delilah had postponed her wedding plans, much to Gus's relief, and was spending whatever time she could steal away from the kitchen with Benjie. The youngster had become withdrawn and had regressed alarmingly, according to Dr. Rossi's latest reports. Jan had relinquished her care of Benjie to Delilah because the boy seemed to become even more sullen and uncooperative whenever she was around. As much as she wanted to believe that this was a temporary state of affairs between her brother and herself, Jan was plagued with concern.

As she took care of the paperwork at the desk in the lobby, Jan's eyes fell on the calender near her elbow. Her heart thumped painfully when the red circled date denoting the wedding date leapt out at her. She had neither seen nor heard from Derek since that morning in the kitchen when Neil told him he would be taking Benjie for his regular visits to the medical center. Out of sight, out of mind, she thought wistfully.

Even before she saw him, Jan picked up the heavy scent of Neil's cologne. He approached the desk and said encouragingly, "It's two o'clock. You are ready to go riding, aren't you?"

If there was one thing she didn't feel like doing, it was going riding with Neil, but she had promised and she would have to honor that promise. Besides, it was time she had a long talk with Neil and found out exactly what his plans were. The past few days everything concerning the tall blond man annoyed her, and she found herself hoping that each day would be his last on her Rancho. The thought made her feel guilty, and she smiled to let him know she was ready to leave with him. "I'm ready whenever you are. Benjie is in the Jacuzzi so I have a little free time."

"I knew that, so I saddled the horses and have them out by the paddock waiting for us. Come on, slowpoke, get a move on," Neil joked.

"You go ahead. I want to change into riding boots and I'll meet you in a few minutes." Neil banged out the screen door and Jan added a column of figures before she closed her ledger and headed toward the stairs and her room.

Looking neither to the right nor the left, Jan crossed the lobby and walked smack into Derek Bannon. It took only one glance for her to see that he was furious to the point of rage.

"You little fool, do you have any idea what you've done?" he demanded coldly. "Do you have any idea at all?"

"Let go of me!" Jan said, frightened by the viselike grip he had on her arm. "What are you talking about?"

"What am I talking about? Don't you know? Are you so blind and wrapped up in your rhinestone cowboy that you've lost sight of what's happening to Ben? Open your eyes! Look at your brother and tell me what you see!"

Frightened by his fury, Jan could only stare at Derek. She could feel her knees tremble and the pain in her arm from his grip was tooth rattling. "What are you talking about?" she repeated.

"I'm talking about Ben and the phone call I received from Dr. Rossi. He tells me Ben has regressed almost to the point he was at when he first began attending the clinic. He chewed me out for neglecting the boy. He also said that when I start something I should finish it and that I had no right to play around with a child's life. Are you listening to me, Jan Warren? Do you hear me? Dr. Rossi said Ben isn't responding to the therapy and he has no desire or will to walk again. He said Ben gave up. Now," Derek said angrily, shaking her arm so viciously that her head almost snapped, "I want you to tell me what's going on, and then I'm going to tell you what I'm going to do."

Jan was terrified both by his verbal and physical onslaught. "Dr. Rossi told me several days ago that Benjie had a setback. That he was regressing. He said he was optimistic and would continue with the treatments. Benjie is...Benjie isn't very happy. He missed you. I knew you would do this to him. You don't care about him. If you did, you would have come around to see how he was doing. Regardless of who takes Benjie for his therapy, you never should have deserted him the way you did. Also, I thought when you found out I wasn't going to sell the Rancho that you didn't want to be bothered with either Benjie or me. I thought..."

"Do me a favor, Miss Warren—don't think. I can't afford it when you think. From now on I'll be taking Ben for his treatments, and if that neon sign that poses as your engaged-to-be-engaged boyfriend interferes, his lights are going to be punched out! When I start something, I finish it. Now where the hell is Ben?"

"He's...he's out in the Jacuzzi. He still has five minutes to go and I think..."

"I've told you, don't think!" Derek snapped "Even Delilah has more sense than you do. Feebleminded..." The rest of his words were lost on Jan as Derek made his way to the pool.

Jan stood on the side and wanted to die at the look on Benjie's face when he saw Derek stoop down on his heels. "I knew you wouldn't forget me! What are you doing here? How come you came? How are all the guys at the Lasso? Gee, Derek, I missed you. How long can you stay?" Benjie babbled nonstop.

"Whoa. One question at a time. From now on I'm back to taking you for your therapy. What in the world made you think I could forget my good buddy? I had some business that needed my attention. I came to see you. The guys miss you, and Dusty said I was to bring you back for the barbecue tonight. I missed you too, Ben. So what do you say? Shake off the water—your time is up. Let's make tracks for the Lasso. There's a lot of your friends who are eager to see you."

"Just you and me, Derek?" Benjie asked hopefully as he waited for Derek's reply.

"You got it—just you and me. Andrea and the guys will be at the barbecue, but with a little luck we can shake them easily enough. Between the two of us, we should be able to handle it."

"Wow! I can't wait! Derek, I haven't been doing so good with Dr. Rossi. I didn't make any... progress since you left."

"I heard about it and I'm here to see that you get back on the track."

"I can't get out of the Jacuzzi by myself. I can't do anything by myself anymore," Benjie said quietly, his blue eyes solemn, the dancing lights that had been there when he first saw Derek extinguished.

"I guess I can help you this time around. Starting tomorrow, though, you're on your own."

Jan watched with a catch in her throat as Derek bent down and lifted Benjie from the Jacuzzi and wrapped the boy in a thirsty towel. Carefully, as though he were handling eggs, he settled the little boy in his wheelchair and bellowed for Delilah. "Dress him and bring him back here. Ten minutes," he thundered.

Derek Bannon made no move in Jan's direction but stood glaring at her in stony silence. His eyes clearly said all, and she knew the words. Hadn't she been saying them to herself over and over these past few days? She had neglected Benjie. She had refused to see what was happening to the little boy. She had been so wrapped up in the ranch and fending off Neil that she had neglected the most important person in her life. If it hadn't been for Derek, how long would she have allowed it to continue? She had no defense; there was no defense. Her shoulders drooped as she headed for Benjie's room.

As Jan turned and walked away, she had half expected Derek to call out to her, to rail her out, to yell and holler, but he hadn't. Why should he? There was no sign that he even knew she was visible.

Delilah was just wheeling Benjie through the door when Jan got to his room. Gus waited patiently for Delilah to help Benjie dress so he could carry him back down the stairs.

"I heard you were going to the Lasso for a barbecue. Have a good time, Benjie," Jan said, her eyes brimming with tears.

"Are you crying because I'm leaving?" Benjie asked in surprise.

"Heck, no. I think I have some kind of allergy."

"Yup," Delilah muttered from where she rummaged through Benjie's dresser for a shirt. "Me get allergy, too. Whenever the dude with the big hat come around. He make my eyes water, too," the woman sniffed.

"Derek says the desert is the best place for allergies. Derek is finished with his business and he's going to take me for my therapy again, starting tomorrow. It's okay, isn't it?" he said anxiously.

"You bet it is," Jan said, blowing her nose.

"Jan, if Derek asks me to sleep over, can I? He said there's a guest room and it's got my name on the door. Can I, Jan? I never did before, because I didn't want you to be alone. Your friend is here, so, if he asks me this time, can I stay?"

Jan was aware of two things—one, that Benjie really did care for her and was concerned about her, and the other, that he still never called Neil by name but always referred to him as "her" friend.

"I think it's a great idea. I know you're going to have a good time. Give me a call, though, just so I know your plans. Okay? I'll be fine. You'd better get a move on. I heard Mr. Bannon give you ten minutes and you're on overtime right now." Quickly, she gave Benjie a peck on the cheek.

Later, Neil found Jan leaning against the wall outside the kitchen door. Tears were streaming down her cheek, but he didn't seem to notice. "Do you have any idea what time it is? I've been stand-

ing out there with two saddled horses for over half
an hour and I feel like a fool! Are you going riding
or not?" he demanded arrogantly.

"Shut up, Neil. Shut up and don't say another
word," Jan cried as she ran into the lodge and
slammed the door shut behind her. Up in her room,
she threw herself on her bed and buried her face in
her pillow.

The soft, velvety night enveloped Jan as she
strolled the grounds of the Rancho Arroyo. For the
second time in days she made a decision to sell the
ranch to Derek Bannon. She knew now she could
never live in such close proximity to Derek and still
survive emotionally. Today had been proof of that
fact. Instead of calling Derek, she would write him
a formal business letter and spell out the terms for
him. She would be asking his original offer, not the
elevated, inflated price he had offered when he
thought she was being plain stubborn.

If Derek didn't want the property or had changed
his mind, then she would have to sell it to someone
else. Surely there were other businessmen who
would be interested in the Rancho for investment
purposes.

She would have to work something out with the
hospital and Dr. Rossi as far as Benjie's treatments
were concerned. Jan's anger rose and her sense of
justice was assaulted. It was fine for Derek to storm

into the ranch and tell her he was taking over Benjie's treatments again because she had sloughed off on her job. But what and who was going to take care of Benjie while Derek was away on his thirty-day honeymoon in Europe? I'll just bet he never gave *that* a thought, Jan sniffed.

A deep feeling of loneliness swept over her. Why couldn't someone fall in love with her and cherish her the way the heroes did in books? She wasn't ugly; she'd been told she had a pleasing personality. Was she unaware of something about herself that was a definite turnoff as far as men were concerned? Men, she said to herself. Be honest; when you talk about men, you're thinking only of Derek Bannon.

A deep sob rose in her throat and she squelched it immediately. No more crying, she told herself firmly.

How bright the stars were. It was a beautiful night, a night made for lovers and close embraces. Someday she would have another night like this and someone special to share it with her.

"Jan, I've been looking all over for you," Neil's voice called from somewhere deep in the shadows. "I want to talk to you."

From where she stood Jan picked up the excitement in Neil's voice. What now? she groaned inwardly.

Neil emerged into the flickering lights that surrounded the pool and motioned for Jan to sit down on a yellow chaise. "I have something I want to tell you," he said exuberantly.

"That's good. Because I have something I want to tell you," Jan said quietly.

"Whatever it is, it can wait. This is important. Jan, I want you to marry me! I've just discovered something that will make us millionaires. Are you listening?"

"Of course I'm listening, and so is half the Rancho. Lower your voice, please," Jan admonished.

Neil's voice dropped a tone. "Jan, don't sell the ranch to Bannon. I found out why he wants it. We can beat him to the punch and do it ourselves and make a fortune."

Jan laughed. He hadn't even bothered to wait for a reply to his marriage proposal. She raised her eyes heavenward and grinned. "This isn't exactly what I had in mind when I prayed for someone to love and cherish me," she mumbled almost silently.

"What did you say?" Neil questioned. "Never mind. Listen. Don't sell Bannon the Rancho."

"What? How did you know? I never told you Derek wanted to buy the Rancho..."

"I know, I know. I overheard you talking to him on the phone..."

"You what?" Jan hissed, starting to rise from her chair. "You spied on me? That's despicable..."

Neil pushed her back down onto the chaise. "Look, there's no time for that now. I know about it and that's all that counts. But don't do it, Jan. We'll take over his plans and make ourselves a fortune. Today I took a run over to the shopping center for some shaving supplies, and there's an architect's office right next to the drugstore. And whose car do you think was parked right outside? Your friend Bannon's. There were some rolled-up blueprints on the front seat and I sort of took a look at them. Don't worry, he doesn't know anything about it. I saw him go into the drugstore with Benjie."

"You what?" Jan demanded, fury lighting her eyes to shards of green glass.

"Shut up. Let me finish. I saw those blueprints, and believe me when I tell you that Bannon is out to steal this place right out of your hands. You can't sell it to him."

"Don't you mean you spied on Derek Bannon, and you spied on me, too? You didn't just happen to see the blueprints—you spied. You should be ashamed of yourself!"

"Well, I'm not!" Neil answered loftily. "It's Bannon who should be ashamed for what he's trying to pull over on you. Well, I won't let him do it to you, to us. I'll pull the rug from under him and we'll roll in clover from now on."

"Neil, I don't love you. I don't want to marry you. Stop saying 'us.'"

Jan's words penetrated and made an impression. "Okay, then I'll be your business manager. We'll clean up," he said, rubbing his hands together. "Say, you didn't even ask what the plans were. Don't you care? Oh, I see. You really don't care and you'll leave it up to me."

"You're right about one thing—I don't care. Listen, Neil, I'm selling the Rancho to Derek Bannon for his original offer. I have no intention of gouging him or keeping this place. I have to do what's best for Benjie and myself. I can't worry about you or Mr. Bannon. I really am tired, Neil, so, if you'll excuse me, I'll go up to bed and you can go back to the Golden Lasso and your nocturnal prowling. By the way, you're going to have to vacate the bunkhouse. Andy Stone will be discharged from the hospital over the weekend, and he'll need his bunk. All the cabins are either filled or reserved, so you'll have to vamoose. You should be able to get a room at the Lasso. Sorry," she said, getting up from the chaise.

Neil appeared stunned but recovered rapidly. "I don't believe what I'm hearing," he snapped. "This guy is out to rip you off and you tell me to move out, when all I have is your best interests at heart?

He's going to build some kind of treatment center for cripples like Benjie. How do you like that? If you keep this place and do the same thing, you could make a fortune. Do you know how easy it is to apply for federal aid? Everybody's got a soft heart when it comes to crippled kids. We could make a fortune just skimming off the top. You're a fool, Jan. I can't believe you're selling out! You could have a gold mine here. Open your eyes!"

Jan's face froze into shocked lines. Could she believe what she was hearing? One look at Neil's determined features told her. "You are the most despicable man I've ever known," she hissed. "You can't stand the sight of Benjie because he's disabled, and yet you'd make the Rancho into a treatment center for children just like Benjie and then steal from them! Get back under your rock, Neil. I want you to clear out of here before morning."

"Listen, Jan. I've put up with a lot from both Benjie and you, and I'm not going to let you go until you see things my way!"

"You don't know *my* way, Neil," she said savagely, lifting her hand and slapping him soundly across his hated face.

"Why, you little . . . !" Instantly, Neil was on his feet, dragging her up with him and holding her fast. "You love him, don't you? You think if you sell the Rancho to him that will make him come around. I've seen him at the Lasso. Women follow him as though he were the pied piper. He's the kind of man who takes everything and leaves nothing behind but tatters and frayed ends. You aren't his type." Neil's voice had become shrill.

Jan struggled for her release, her fingers curling into claws reaching for his face. "I know one thing, Neil—Derek Bannon doesn't steal. If his plan is to make a treatment center for handicapped children, it isn't with the intention of skimming off the top. Regardless of his romantic adventures, he's a man of honor and principle. But, then, you wouldn't know anything about that, would you?"

"You're not going to cheat me out of this, Jan. This is the chance of a lifetime, and you're not going to stop me!" Unleashing his rage, Neil tossed her backward, knocking her off balance and throwing her down into the chaise. She saw him lift his arm, his hand bunched into a fist, ready to strike her.

Suddenly, a figure stepped out from the path and seized Neil's arm. Derek Bannon. Neil turned with fury upon Derek, now aiming his blow upon him. Derek blocked, stopping Neil's fist in midair, and directed a well-placed blow to Neil's midsection. As Neil doubled over to clutch his stomach, Derek pounded his fist into Neil's face, knocking him backward onto the grass.

"Now, get up and get out of here; you heard the lady! And don't ever show your face around these parts again!" Derek's voice was harsh, filled with menace and fury.

Neil touched his hand to his nose and mouth, and his fingers came away stained with his own blood.

Stunned by Derek's sudden violence, Jan stood abruptly and loomed over Neil's reclining figure. "I've told you once and I'll tell you again—this time for the last time. Go back under your rock, Neil—that's where you belong." Unable to stomach the sight of him for another instant, she turned on her heel, squared her shoulders, and headed for the lodge.

Derek caught up with her on the veranda and held the door open for her. "I just came by to tell you Benjie is staying the night with me. He's with Dusty and the guys right now. I tried calling you, but Delilah said you were outside somewhere. I came by hoping to find you."

Why was he looking at her that way? Had he heard her defense of him to Neil? Or had he just happened upon them just as Neil was about to strike her? Even if he had heard, what difference did it make? It couldn't matter to him; he was going to marry Andrea in just a few days. "Good night, Derek. Thank you for going to all this trouble to tell me about Benjie."

"Jan, wait. I want to talk to you." Derek gripped her wrist, stopping her hasty retreat.

"Regardless of what you want, Derek, I've had enough. E-N-O-U-G-H! Go back where you belong and I'll stay where I belong." He reached for her, his hand cupping her chin, forcing her gaze to meet his. Desperately, Jan tried to avoid his penetrating stare. In agonizing defeat she knew she was helpless against him. Slowly—ever so slowly—she raised her eyes to meet his. The past few minutes had been too emotionally charged. She had discovered so much, and yet there were so many mysterious shadows remaining. She admitted it hadn't been so great a shock to discover what a heel Neil Connors was. Hadn't she always suspected it, based on the way he treated Benjie? And it hadn't really come as a devastating revelation to learn that Derek intended to use the Rancho Arroyo as a camp for handicapped children. Hadn't she learned about his generosity at the medical center? But, still, it was all becoming too much to handle. It was the havoc her own emotions created within her that was bringing tears to her eyes. Derek touched his finger to the glistening tear as it raced along her smooth cheek.

"You're coming with me," he stated simply, pulling her across the porch and pushing her into his station wagon, which was parked out in front of the lodge.

All the fight had gone out of her. Somehow she knew that her protests would fall on deaf ears, and she was so tired. So very tired. Drained emotionally. Obedient to his demands, she allowed herself to be put into the car and sat quietly as he climbed in beside her and spurred the engine to life.

The night was black, the only light coming from the headlights as they drove along the road leading to the interstate highway. Jan cowered against the door, too numbed to wonder where he was taking her, too defeated to even ask.

Just before the turnoff for the interstate, Derek swung the long station wagon onto a side road and parked. The lights from the dashboard struck his features, turning his eyes dark and delineating his chiseled jaw. His dark hair was tousled and falling across his forehead, lending him a boyish look. But his mouth was grim, tight—little more than a thin line of anger.

"Now will you tell me what this is all about? What goes on in that silly head of yours? Jan," he said in exasperation, "sometimes I feel as though we're so close. Then suddenly, without warning, something comes between us and I don't understand it. I know you feel something for me. You proved that the day we were in Dr. Rossi's barn."

Jan was silent, refusing to answer. What did he want her to do? What did he want her to say? He had no right to bring her here, to corner her, to demand she confess she loved him when in a few days he would be marrying someone else. Or was that his little game? Did his male ego demand she throw herself at his feet and plead and beg with him not to marry Andrea? Never! She warned herself. Regardless of how close and tempting those words were to her lips. She would never beg. How could he not know that his relationship with Andrea was the only thing that kept her from throwing herself into his arms and declaring her love?

"Jan?" His voice was so close it startled her. Suddenly his arms were around her, pulling her closer. His lips found the soft skin below her ear and his breath was warm and stirred her senses as he whispered, "Don't pull away, Jan..." and then his mouth covered hers and blocked out the universe.

Jan was moved by his plea. How could she deny him anything? This was Derek, the man she loved. She relaxed against him, her head tipped upward and resting against his shoulder. She felt the feather-light caress of his lips on her hair. "You always smell so sweet," he murmured as he bent his head, searching once again for her lips.

Her arms slid around him, aware of his hard-muscled torso against her touch. Unconsciously, her hands wound around him, hugging him closer. Derek kissed her, a warm, searching, drugging kiss, teasing Jan's senses and licking the flames of passion that were banked within her. Slow to passion, deliciously slow, touching, tender, loving, adoring...his lips traced a pattern that evoked her response.

His hands took possession of her, roaming lazily over her body, molding her to him. And he breathed her name, so softly she thought she had only imagined hearing it.

Her parted lips followed the strong line of his jaw and descended to the hollow of his neck. She gave herself up to the pressure of his touch on her body, feeling as though the world began and ended within the circle of his embrace.

The night was dark; the moment was rapture. Derek held her tenderly, quieting his passions, yet arousing her own. And when she felt his fingers fumbling with the buttons on her blouse, she made no protest. Being with him, loving him seemed the most natural thing in the world.

His touch against her skin ignited a spark that blossomed into a shower of flames. The sound of her name on his lips before he covered hers was as heady as imported brandy. And the air was sweet and the night was silent. Only the whisper of his name rode on the desert breeze.

And when he followed the curve of her chin along her throat and touched his lips to the hollow between her breasts, she arched her back, welcoming his touch. Within her burned the new sensation of an indescribable budding, a splintering emotion that swelled and bounded from deep within her.

When she heard it, she thought it was merely wishful thinking. But he said it again—this time louder, hesitantly, as though unsure of her response. "I love you, Jan."

The words that she longed to hear and should have made her the happiest woman alive instead broke the magic. Jan's spine stiffened and he sensed her immediate withdrawal.

Puzzled, he sat back, looking at her as she struggled with shaking fingers to redo her buttons. Softly, so softly she had to strain to hear him, he said, "I thought you wanted me to love you, Jan."

Jan's eyes flashed with fury. "To repeat one of your own phrases, Mr. Bannon, you shouldn't think! Now, take me home!"

She was angry, angrier than she'd ever been in her life. Derek had no right to do these things to her! He had no right to tell her he loved her—not with Andrea waiting for him up at the Golden Lasso!

Without another word, Derek started the car and expertly maneuvered it around and onto the secondary road leading to the Rancho. Although he was silent, when Jan sneaked a peek at him she saw his features were stricken. He gripped the steering wheel with a fury that whitened his knuckles. She couldn't think! She wouldn't think! She wouldn't be Derek Bannon's new plaything until something better came his way. And what of his wife-to-be?

Jan never imagined that she would find cause to pity the beautiful Andrea, but at this moment that was exactly what she did.

A few moments later Derek drove the station wagon up to the front of the lodge. An instant before Jan found the door handle Derek turned to face her. His features were stiff with rage and his voice, when he spoke, was rife and menace. "Get out of my car, Miss Warren. I'll do my best to forget what a fool I made of myself tonight, and I hope you'll have the decency to do the same. Get out."

Jan was paralyzed by the menace in his tone and the naked hatred in his face. "Decency!" she cried. He had already turned his head away from her and his foot pressed the accelerator and revved the engine impatiently. Exasperated beyond words, Jan sprung from the car and slammed the door shut, hearing the window rattle and wishing it would shatter into a million pieces. It would be fitting. That's exactly what her heart felt like—as though Derek Bannon had crushed it in his hands and shattered it into a million pieces.

Chapter Thirteen

Jan descended the stairs early the next morning and pasted a stiff smile on her face. There was no sense in parading around with her heart on her sleeve for all the hands to see. The night had been interminably long and lonely. Thoughts of Derek kept turning over and over in her head, denying her peace and stealing her sleep. And when she did fall asleep, finally, it was only to awaken with a start, expecting to find him there beside her, whispering her name and holding her close. She must put it all behind her now, push it out of her mind and out of her life. But all through the night she heard him whisper, "I love you, Jan," and yet the dreaded vision of the naked hatred on his face as he ordered her out of his car returned to confound her.

Quickly, she entered the kitchen where Delilah was busy at the stove while the ranch hands stood in line waiting for her to drop a stack of wheat cakes onto their plates.

After saying good morning, Jan poured herself a cup of coffee and looked inquiringly at Delilah. "When did you start humming to yourself in the morning?"

"When your friend make tracks in the night."

"Neil?"

"*Tsk, tsk, tsk*—you have only one friend. Yes, rhinestone cowboy leave early this morning. Not even leave one rhinestone behind. Is good, yes?" Delilah grinned, showing her strong white teeth.

"Is good, yes," Jan mimicked. "But I'm not surprised. He received his walking papers last night."

"Yes. And also he got something else," Delilah said as she served another ranch hand. "Your friend got himself one swollen lip, two loose teeth, and banged-up nose. Right, fellas?" She addressed the four men sitting at the long table, devouring her luscious wheat cakes.

"Right!" they called in unison.

Jan grimaced, Neil had lived with the hands and yet he had been unable to become friends with any of them. That had a lot to say about the man.

"Wonder who punched your friend out?" Delilah muttered. "Me? I not give him time of day."

Hmmm. I wonder." Jan pretended bafflement.

"Sometimes I think you maybe not so dumb as you look," Delilah said heartily. "You just take longer than most."

Jan gulped. "I'll take that as a compliment and leave the rest unsaid." She grimaced. "How's breakfast coming? Need any help?"

"No, you sit down and eat. You too skinny—like stick!"

Jan took her place at the table and picked at a breakfast plate that Delilah had put in front of her. Should she tell everyone that she was selling the ranch to Derek Bannon? Should she wait? No. It wouldn't be fair. It was important to everyone to know her plans so they wouldn't be left high and dry at the last minute. She was glad Benjie wasn't here to hear it like this. She would have to handle him very delicately when she broke the news.

When breakfast was over and some of the men broke out cigarettes, Jan called for their attention. "I have something to tell everyone and I hope you'll understand. You all know the unexpected expenses we've been faced with lately; it's been difficult keeping the ranch in the black. Matter of fact, there were several times I thought we would go under. Also, there's the competition from the Golden Lasso to contend with, and that's not easy. We just can't afford to offer the accommodations they offer there. So—" she took a deep breath, "—I've decided to take Derek Bannon's offer and sell him the Rancho." There, she had said it, but she hadn't expected the crestfallen faces of her staff.

There was silence. Total and complete.

"Listen, everyone. It's not what you think. I haven't given up and I'm not selling out for a higher price. As a matter of fact, I'm accepting Mr. Bannon's first offer. I believe him when he said that Uncle Jake died before he could sign the necessary papers. But I do know this. He's going to need help. Mr. Bannon isn't just going to make this Rancho a part of the Golden Lasso and use it for his staff's living quarters. I've discovered he wants to open a treatment center for handicapped children. He'll be needing all the help he can get."

"Miss Warren, is there anything we can do to help you change your mind? We hate to see you leave and we'll miss Ben. We really care about that kid, and you, too." It was the first time Gus had said more than five or six words.

"Gus, no, I'm sorry. I just can't handle it financially. Sooner or later it would have to come to this and it would have been even more difficult. I've got to secure Benjie's future and I can't do that if I have to file for bankruptcy. Understand? And I would appreciate it if none of you mentioned this to Benjie. I'll find the right time to tell him."

There were mutters and finally agreements around the table. It was heartwarming to know that in a few short months she had come to be so well thought of at the Rancho. The atmosphere was dismal, subdued to the point of a funeral.

Groping for something to lighten the mood, Jan turned to Delilah. "When are you and Gus getting married?"

Delilah shrugged.

"What do you say we have the wedding here? You could invite all your friends, and it would really be something for our guests to attend. And the Rancho will empty out its food locker to feed everyone. What do you say, Delilah?"

"I say you too late. Gus and me get married yesterday afternoon in Presbyterian church."

Gus stood up from his place at the table and raised his coffee mug. "To Delilah." He offered the toast to his new bride. Then, in a most unexpected display of affection, he rounded the table, caught

Delilah in his arms, and squeezed her tightly. With a resounding smack, he put a kiss on her chubby cheek. Everyone praised Gus for his choice in women and immediately the mood lightened.

Jan smiled brightly, but inside she was dreading the thought of telling Benjie of her decision to sell the Rancho. He had come to love these people just as she had. It was cruel, but, then, life was cruel. She, too, had come to love someone, and she knew the pain of not being able to be near him. She would weather it; she would have to. And so would Benjie.

Jan closeted herself in her office to accomplish two things. One was that she would manage to avoid Benjie's eyes when he returned from the Golden Lasso with Derek; and, two, it would give her an opportunity to discuss selling the Rancho with her uncle's lawyer.

As she was on the phone with the lawyer, she heard Derek's powerful sports car pull up the drive. Gus went out to help Benjie, who was looking marvelously improved. The boy was using his crutches again and he refused Gus's helping hand. Derek had remained in the car with the motor running. As Benjie waved goodbye, he shouted something that sounded like "See you at the wedding!"

For a moment Jan was so distracted that the lawyer had to repeat something twice before she heard him. "Just draw up the papers and I'll come into town next week to sign them. Anything, as long as it isn't necessary for me to come face to face with Derek Bannon."

If the lawyer thought this a strange request, he didn't say so, he just muttered something about wanting to play golf this weekend, and now he was going to have all this paperwork.

Jan buried herself in the ledgers and receipts and bills. A few minutes later, Benjie knocked on the office door and entered. "Hey, Jan, Derek's gonna pick me up to take me to the medical center in about two minutes. I asked him to wait around for me when he dropped me off, but he said he had something to do up at the Lasso. Why don't you come out and say hello to him when he comes for me?"

Jan looked up at Benjie's bright blue eyes. Derek Bannon had worked his magic on the little boy once again. "I can't come out, Benjie—I've got so much work to do."

"Aw, come on out, Jan. It won't take but a minute. Please, Jan?"

Unable to deny Benjie this one small request in the face of the news about selling the Rancho, Jan smiled. "Okay, sport. I'll wait on the veranda for you."

The midmorning air was already heavy and hot, but it was a balm to Jan, who, ever since Derek had dropped her off the night before, felt as though she could never be warm again. Benjie prattled something about the preparations for the wedding, and Jan only half listened, insulating herself against the pain. From Benjie's report, the florists were already decorating a small dining room that would serve as the chapel, and the cooks were preparing the most scrumptious food Benjie had ever seen. The boy's eyes widened as he described the ice sculpture of turtle doves that would be used for the champagne fountain. "It's really something, Jan. I bet you've never seen anything like it! Andrea says that the man had to come all the way from California to do it!"

Smiling stiffly, Jan tried to show enthusiasm for the news Benjie was reporting. The last thing she wanted to hear about was Andrea's wedding plans and the elaborate showing she and Derek were planning to make. *"I love you, Jan."* The words seemed to float on the desert wind. *"I love you, Jan."* The remembered tone of Derek's voice as he whispered those words sent Jan into a panic. Nervously, she turned to Benjie, asking him inane questions about the medical clinic, Dr. Rossi, the Bison football team—anything to blot out the wound of those words.

"What's the matter with you, sis? You're as jumpy as a cat on a griddle." Benjie questioned her, piercing her with his stare.

"Nothing," she snapped. "I thought you wanted me to come out here and keep you company. I'm keeping you company!" she insisted, hearing her own voice rise two octaves.

As though saved by the bell, Derek's car rounded the drive. He honked his horn and Benjie hurried out to the car on his crutches. "I won't be needing these before long," he called out to Jan. "Someday I'm just going to run off that porch and right over to Derek!"

The conviction in the boy's voice convinced Jan. If nothing else, she had to be grateful to Derek Bannon for her brother's bright prognosis.

The whole time Benjie was settling himself in the car, Derek kept his face turned away. It seemed as though Derek had spoken the truth about feeling like a fool the night before. Well, it served him right. But in her heart Jan knew there was no bigger fool than she. The sight of Derek's head turned away from her ate at her soul. She had to hurry the lawyer, do everything she could to facilitate the deal about selling the Rancho. She had to get away from here, away from the desert, away from Derek Bannon. Her heart beat thunderously in her breast, her breath caught in her throat, and tears stung her eyes. Heaven help her, whatever the man was, whatever he did, she loved him. *"I love you, Jan."*

The fickle desert wind had returned his words again. *"I love you, Jan."*

"Come on, Jan! You're gonna make us late!" Benjie admonished through the closed bedroom door.

"I'm coming. Just a minute!" she answered, desperately trying to keep her voice light.

"You said that ten minutes ago! Come on!"

"All right, all right! Just give me a few more minutes without your badgering. Now get away from the door and wait for me in the lobby. I'm hurrying."

Jan sighed deeply as she stroked the brush through her hair. She felt as though she were marching to her own execution. Today was going to be the worst day of her life. First, she was being forced to attend Andrea's wedding; and second, she was going to have to tell Benjie of her decision to sell the Rancho.

There was no avoiding it. The boy had to know. And the longer she put it off, the harder it would be on him.

Jan surveyed herself in front of the pier glass, checking her hem and the back of the pale blue linen dress she had decided to wear. If she had to watch the man she loved marry someone else, at least it would be while looking her best. Her cinnamon-colored hair shone, and there was just the right amount of color in her cheeks. The linen sheath dress hugged her hips and emphasized her long, lean legs. Satisfied that everything was where it should be, she hurried out of her room and down the stairs into the lobby.

Benjie emitted a long, low whistle, which caused Jan to raise her brows. "Where did you learn a thing like that?" she demanded. "Riding through town with Derek, no doubt." Her tone was harsher than she intended and Benjie looked at her curiously. "Don't look at me like that," she scolded. "You were the one in a hurry. Now, let's get going."

Even as they drove through the gates of the Golden Lasso, it was evident there was a festive note in the air. Garlands of flowers lined the drive, and crepe-paper wedding bells were entwined around the lamp posts. A parking attendant, resplendent in livery, claimed Jan's pickup truck and drove it around to the back lot. Benjie was impatient and became insistent when he heard the organ music coming from the small back dining room. "I told you you would make us late! Now hurry up or I'm gonna leave you here!"

The last thing Jan wanted was to have to enter the makeshift chapel all by herself, so she hurried behind Benjie, who was making fast tracks for the chapel.

Inside the chapel soft organ music played the Wedding March. The interior was decorated with hundreds of flowers and white satin ribbons. The center aisle had been overlayed with a white carpet that led to the makeshift altar where Andrea and Derek would pronounce their vows.

Jan's eyes became misty and her throat choked up. How could she sit here and watch Derek swear his love for Andrea when only a few days ago he had whispered those words to her. A great heaviness weighed on Jan's heart. Her impulse was to run—run away as fast and as far as she could. Instead, she sat there paralyzed, incapable of motion, knowing only that the one man she could ever love was standing there at the altar waiting for his bride.

"Derek looks great in his penguin suit, doesn't he?" Benjie whispered.

"What?"

"His tuxedo. Derek calls it a penguin. And, hey, doesn't Dusty look nervous?"

"Shh!"

The organist began the Wedding March again, and the outer doors swung open to reveal two pretty girls dressed in yellow and carrying baskets of flowers. Behind her bridesmaids, Andrea stood, awaiting her cue. Jan caught her breath when she saw the dark-haired girl, who was beautiful in her antique lace gown and fine Holland lace veil.

Suddenly, Derek was standing beside Andrea, murmuring something to her and giving her a slight chuck on the chin. Derek! What was he doing back there? He should have waited for Andrea at the altar!

Benjie was pulling on Jan's arm. "Jan, Jan. When you get married can I give you away like Derek's giving his sister away?"

The full import of Benjie's words didn't penetrate Jan's consciousness for a full minute. Giving his sister away? Andrea was Derek's sister? No! It couldn't be! Jan's thoughts raced backward, trying to remember who had told her that Derek was marrying Andrea. No one. No one had told her.

Back, through the haze of the days . . . Andrea, sitting beside Dusty Baker on the plane, telling him that she was going to be married. That was a flirtation, a coyness. And that time at the Golden Lasso when Dusty Baker introduced Andrea and she had interrupted him, not wanting to hear the words "Derek's fiancée." Jan's eyes followed Andrea and Derek and jumped ahead of them to where Dusty Baker was waiting. Andrea was going to marry Dusty! That was why Derek hadn't been jealous at the tribute dinner. How could he be jealous of his sister?

Back again, to where she had seen Andrea hug Derek in the airport. What made her think it had been more than sisterly affection? Had hearing Andrea's words on the plane and her own instant jealousy of the girl colored everything she knew about the girl?

And of course Andrea lived with Derek. Where else should she live while waiting to be married? Andrea had had every right to answer the door in the middle of the night wearing her nightgown.

Fool! Fool! Fool! she cursed herself. Always jumping to conclusions. The agony she had caused herself thinking Derek was in love with Andrea. The pain she had inflicted on everyone because she had assumed that Andrea was going to marry Derek!

Derek! Jan's heart leaped in her breast. Derek had said he loved her. *"I love you, Jan."* Again she heard the words, listened for the warm timbre in his voice. Fool! Fool! What had she done? Her pride had kept her from discovering the truth. All those times when doubt had ruined what it was that she and Derek had between them, all she had had to do was say it. Tell him. Even if she had openly accused him of being engaged to marry Andrea while toying with her emotions—Derek would have laughed and then taken her in his arms and told her that she was such a silly because Andrea was his sister. His sister!

And Andrea, coming to see her when she was laid up with blisters on her feet and offering her friendship again. How many times had she insulted the unwitting girl by rebuffing her offers of friendship? Even now, she couldn't remember Andrea saying or doing one nasty thing to encourage Jan's hostility. No, it had all been Jan.

She covered her face with her hands to stifle her sobs. Benjie was embarrassed and she heard him whisper to someone: "Girls. They always cry at weddings."

Again the music reached a crescendo and filled the chapel with brightness. Andrea raced down the aisle with Dusty, her face as bright as the Arizona sunshine, and Dusty looking as proud as a peacock.

The wedding guests emptied out after the bride and groom, and Jan knew the impulse to turn and run. Fool! Fool!

Leaving Benjie behind, she followed the crush of guests out into the elegantly appointed lobby of the Golden Lasso. Tears streaming down her face, Jan longed for escape. Suddenly, she heard someone call her name.

"Jan!"

She turned to see Andrea standing on the stairs, looking down at her. "Jan! Catch!" The bridal bouquet flew through the air, and with the accuracy of the Bisons' quarterback, Andrea's toss went directly into Jan's arms.

Fresh tears stung Jan's eyes and, clutching the bouquet to her, she ran out of the Lasso and across the wide expanse of lawn. Over and over the words, "Fool, fool!" shrieked through her head, blocking out all other sound.

The remembered sight of the hatred on Derek's face swam before her. She could never make it up to him, not if she lived to be a hundred. The most wonderful man in the world had told her he loved her, and she had destroyed that love, crushed it beyond repair. "Fool! Fool!"

"I love you, Jan."

The words seemed to come from a distance, and yet they were close enough to touch her heart. She turned and saw him walking toward her. Through the mist of her tears, she saw he was smiling. "I see you've caught the bridal bouquet. You know what that means, don't you?"

He was standing beside her, offering her his snowy handkerchief to dry her tears. "Weddings make me cry, too. Especially when it's not my wedding to you, Jan." His voice was gentle, quiet, almost somber.

"Derek, I've been such a fool...you don't know. I thought—I thought—"

She was in his arms, her heart beating fast against his. His eyes held the sky as he looked down at her and a smile played near the corner of his mouth. "Kiss me. Tell me that you love me. To coin a phrase, Jan—don't think."

And she didn't as he held her tighter and gently parted her lips with his own, robbing her mind of all thought except him.

* * * * *